Dear Romance Reader,

Welcome to a world of breathtaking passion and never-ending romance.

Welcome to *Precious Gem Romances.*

It is our pleasure to present *Precious Gem Romances,* a wonderful new line of romance books by some of America's best-loved authors. Let these thrilling historical and contemporary romances sweep you away to far-off times and places in stories that will dazzle your senses and melt your heart.

Sparkling with joy, laughter, and love, each *Precious Gem Romance* glows with all the passion and excitement you expect from the very best in romance. Offered at a great affordable price, these books are an irresistible value—and an essential addition to your romance collection. Tender love stories you will want to read again and again. *Precious Gem Romances* are books you will treasure forever.

Look for eight fabulous new *Precious Gem Romances* each month—available only at Wal★Mart.

Lynn Brown, Publisher

MASQUERADE

Kathryn Hockett

ZEBRA BOOKS
KENSINGTON PUBLISHING CORP.

This book is dedicated to my very best friend, Julie Munoz, a very special lady who is always there when I need her. Thank you for listening, for caring, and for just being there all the times when my heart was breaking.

ZEBRA BOOKS are published by

Kensington Publishing Corp.
850 Third Avenue
New York, NY 10022

Copyright © 1996 by Kathryn Kramer

All rights reserved. No part of this book may be reproduced in any form or by any means without the prior written consent of the Publisher, excepting brief quotes used in reviews.

If you purchased this book without a cover, you should be aware that this book is stolen property. It was reported as "unsold and destroyed" to the Publisher and neither the Author nor the Publisher has received any payment for this "stripped book."

Zebra and the Z logo Reg. U.S. Pat. & TM Off.

First Printing: August, 1996
10 9 8 7 6 5 4 3 2 1

Printed in the United States of America

Whoso loves,
Believes the impossible.

—Elizabeth Barrett Browning, "Aurora Leigh"

AUTHOR'S NOTE

During the period when Victoria was Queen of England, Great Britain became the strongest and richest nation of the world. Its empire included colonies in almost every part of the world, extending over an area five times the size of Europe. The country's prestige was enormous. No power, with the single exception of Russia, ventured to challenge her during this period. Britain, with her unbeaten Navy, towered above all rivals.

It was claimed that the age stood for peace and prosperity. Victorian art, architecture, and interior decoration show a desire for large size and fancy designs that glorify the vastness and wealth of the British Empire. The heroes and heroines in Victorian novels are sedate and prim, reflecting the strict morals of the time. On the surface all seemed calm, yet the age we now call "Victorian" was marked by intense, often dramatic changes, social, political, and economic.

The world was undergoing a decisive transformation; mainly the redistribution of population. This constituted an even farther-reaching change as people moved from the country to the cities in search of work and prosperity. A radical alteration took place in the manner in which men earned their daily bread, as well as in the manner in which they lived.

At first industrialization made it possible for ambitious, thrifty, and hardworking men to improve their daily existence. There were many self-made men who earned their success and bettered their lives. All too soon, however, the towns and cities became ugly, insanitary, and overcrowded, with noisome slums that posed perplexing problems. Jobs became scarcer and opportunities not as plentiful. Long, grueling hours of work, low rates of pay, and neglect of safety precautions in factories and mines became the normal routine of the day. Soon the cities became much like anthills overcrowded to the brim with too many worker ants. Life often became a grim struggle just for a man's very existence. It was all too easy to lose one's way. The statistics of the age state that one person in twelve was a pauper. Soon a disturbing question arose. What should be done about the poor?

Poverty was a grim specter feared by everyone, yet members of society more often than not adopted a callous attitude toward the victims of penury. Unfortunately, the general attitude was that there was some connection between privation and laziness, that the needy were suffering for their own sins and thus had control of their destinies. The truth was that those who had toiled for years could be thrown out of work and thus rendered penniless by old age, illness, or even a slump in business. When this happened they were often thrust heartlessly into a workhouse, separated from their families and compelled to keep company with criminals, lunatics, and prostitutes.

Those who turned their faces away from the needy espoused the philosophy that the cure for poverty was in the hands of the poor themselves, forgetting how thin the line was between thrift and penury. Frequently, there was a contemptuous attitude among the citizens of the city toward those less fortunate than themselves. Indeed, the few charities in existence often had their funds diverted to "private uses."

Wealth and poverty existed side by side. The poor who felt forgotten or scorned all too frequently turned to a life of crime. Those of impeccable morality and position often rubbed elbows with pickpockets and prostitutes on the crowded streets. As a thriving international seaport, London offered rich pickings for those skilled with their fingers. London was much like a chessmatch with only those who could live by their wits coming out the winner. Even so, it was not impossible to raise oneself to a higher standard of living if given the proper opportunity. So it was that two London "sparrows" tried to give fate a hand in earning their fortunes. Both embarked on a masquerade in hopes of bettering their lives, little realizing the danger in playing a game of hearts.

Part One

Two London Sparrows
Orley Square-Autumn, 1850

*There are only two families in the world, the Haves and the
Have Nots.*

—Cervantes, *Don Quixote*

One

It was a morning much like any other, that time when the people of the night were giving way to the people that roamed about in the day. The last drunken man was stumbling along, trying to find his way home before the glare of sunlight tortured his eyes. The night houses were closed. The coach stands deserted. The drunken, the dissipated, and the wretched had disappeared. The more sober and orderly part of the population had awakened. A different kind of personage was making himself known, the worker and the shopkeeper of the city.

As usual, the cobbled streets of London seethed with traffic; wagons, carriages and coaches, sending pedestrians fleeing as they rumbled down the road. Men were shouting, horses neighing, dogs barking, cats fighting. Wheeled vehicles stirred up dust as they rattled by. The walkways of London were a cacophony of sounds as Jamie Morgan strolled along. Blending in with these people of the city was his intent, at least until he'd had time to assess the *pickings* of the day.

James Matthew Morgan was tall and muscular. His dark gray coat hugged broad shoulders, his black trousers clung to long, powerful legs. With his head held high, he walked with a proud gait that made passersby nearly forget the patches that covered his elbows and knees. His hair was thick and dark, just long enough to brush his collar in the back with a hint of curl. His eyes were a vibrant shade of hazel, a mixture between brown and green, dancing with flecks of gold. Jamie Morgan was a handsome man who seemed out of place among the poor of the city, yet that was what he was, as well as a rogue and a thief.

"Good daiy!" With a show of good manners he tipped his faded hat, greeting the women as they walked down the street. Several had straw baskets bulging with fruit that were balanced on their heads or slung over their shoulders offering him a tempting fare for his breakfast. Even so he resisted the chance to use his nimble fingers, knowing instinctively that at least one of the female vendors would capitulate to his smile. Very quickly one did.

"Would you like a pear or pippin, Sir?" A blushing young girl held the prize out to him.

"Indeed I would." Her reward was a slightly wilted pale pink gillyflower that he wore in his lapel.

"Thank you, Sir." She eyed him hopefully as he relished the tartly ripe apple, giggling when he winked.

"It was sweet, it was. Loike you." With grateful appreciation he gently pinched her cheek promising that he would see her again. Then throwing the applecore over his shoulder he continued nonchalantly on his way.

The day had started well, welcoming him with warmth. He had lain in his bed blinking up through the hole in the roof at the scrap of blue sky, relishing the warmth of the early morning rays on his face. Too soon summer would give way to autumn and autumn to the cold of winter, but until it did he'd bask in the sunshine.

Jamie took time to enjoy the morning in all its bustle. He strolled about with the jaunty air of a well-to-do man about town. This was his city, his home. With all its faults he loved London. There was always excitement here, day or night. He pushed his way through the busy, eager crowd, listening to the shouts of men and women calling out their wares, the shrieks of those trying to argue a bargain. Although the noise and chatter assaulted his ears, it all seemed like music. It was good to be alive, to enjoy a certain kind of freedom. To be able to come and go as he pleased. The days he'd spent at the orphanage seemed thankfully distant to him now.

Jamie tensed his jaw and closed his eyes against the pain that memory still caused him. He had suffered from the death of his mother, a poverty-stricken widow who had driven herself beyond endurance into an early grave. Oh, how he had loved her. She had been the only gentleness in a world turned heartless and cruel.

"Don't work so hard, Mum. We'll get by," he had said. But she hadn't really listened. She had taken a job cleaning the houses of the "nobs" during the day and working at a tavern at night. A woman had to work twice as hard as a man to make half as much, or so it seemed.

Basking in the glow of her love, he had been able to put from his mind the shame of his patched and shabby clothing, the cold nights that left him shivering, the aching in his belly when he had to go to bed without supper. Then, just when it seemed there was a silver lining to their cloud after all, she had suddenly grown very thin. Cadaverishly so. Her bones stuck out with little flesh upon them, her eyes were underscored with dark gray shadows.

Consumption the doctor called it, though Jamie knew it by another name. Though his mother told him not to worry Jamie could tell by her rasping breath, the dry cough that shook her thin frame, that she was dying. Even so, he wasn't prepared when the end finally came.

"Mum! Mum!"

He had wept silent, agonized tears as he brushed back the hair from her pale lifeless face. First his father and then his mother. It wasn't fair. Why? He was certain that he would never survive the loneliness and, indeed, he almost didn't. Without his mother, the harshness of reality had come crashing around him. It was as if the bottom had dropped out of his world, as if he were balancing on a precipice that led to total despair.

Alone, penniless, Jamie had been taken to an orphanage, a place that had soon shattered any small remnant of his pride. He was told over and over again of his faults, worked nearly beyond

Kathryn Hockett

his endurance, whipped and lashed and beaten for the slightest departure from the rules. Though he had held the secret hope that someone, anyone, would come and take him away from that dismal place, he was disappointed time after time. He was too old, too dark of hair, too tall to find favor with those coming in search of adoptive children. He was passed over again and again. Cherubic boys and girls with flaxen curls were the ones who were chosen. He had feared there would be no escape.

Reaching up, Jamie brushed a lock of hair from his eyes. He refused to think about it. There was no reason to spoil his tranquil mood. It was a long, long time ago. The ghosts of his past were best forgotten, best put out of his mind. Alas, it was not so easy. Passing by a bakery shop his eyes were drawn to a small group of ragged boys.

"London sparrows," he mumbled beneath his breath.

Their long, thin ankles and large unshapely feet at the end of trousers long outgrown had given them the name. A sparrow, that's what he had once been. Just like those little lads of eight or nine standing with their noses pressed against the bakery window front. Those wretched innocents who grubbed about the streets for victuals in the day and picked up whatever could be found by night. Children whose faces were lined with misery. So much so that they looked more like little old men than boys.

Jamie knew that if not for his own determination and strength of will he too would have known such a fate, left to wander about the streets to pick up a precarious crumb here and there—like a ship adrift in a storm with no port to give haven. He'd been just about nine years of age when he had at last run away from the cruelty and strict uncaring discipline of the orphanage, a wretched outcast with no one to care about him. Like these children he had had that pale, hungry look with a rueful mouth and large sad eyes, at least until the thieves of Orley Square had taken him in. Jamie had quickly learned his trade, earning his own way among his newfound friends.

" 'Ere now. Wot's this?"

The boys crouched around the doorway, holding out their

hands in supplication only to be set upon by an irate shopkeeper. Feeling a twinge of pity Jamie reached in his pocket and came up with a few coins. He'd wanted to use them to purchase his own fare, a steaming cup of tea, a pastry, but his conscience dictated that these urchins had far greater need. He could get more money, and these boys looked as though they were half starving. In a surge of generosity he scattered every one of the coins upon the cobbled stones.

"Here yer go!" He watched as the boys conversed upon the pennies like birds to a handful of crumbs. "Poor little sparrows."

What a sad lot it was for children to have to suffer poverty, they who shared no blame in their fate. Some were the offspring of parents who succumbed to too much gin, a few had been set adrift by their parents to wander the streets, and there were those who, like himself, had been orphaned at an early age or ran away. Well, at least this morning they wouldn't go hungry.

Patting his empty pockets, Jamie shrugged his shoulders. It was time to replenish his stash of coins, though he might have liked to spend a bit more time sauntering the streets amiably. He had to get down to business, his way of making money, as the best pickpocket in all of Orley Square.

Sometimes, in his moments of self-examination, he felt a loathing for the life he was leading—stealing from others—but he quickly brushed it away. Any twinge of guilt he might have felt was washed away by the memory of the time he had spent wandering the streets. No one had offered him comfort or shown any kindness to a boy facing starvation. They had been deaf to his cries, blind to his need. Only the thieves had taken him in.

He quickly assured himself that what he was doing would not lead him on the road to hell. A man had to do what he could to survive. Besides, he had talent. Stealing was an art. Thievery the only way he had of making a living. Thrusting his shoulders back, holding his head high, he continued on his way, spying a likely conquest across the crowded street.

* * *

The warmth of the sun danced down upon the spires and roofs of the city like a shining halo. Even so, Elizabeth Longley kept her white mobcap pulled down tightly over her auburn hair. It was so thick, so unruly at times that she allowed only a few wisps of her waistlength tresses to peek out beneath the muslin, enough to frame her pertly pretty face.

"Violets. Buy my violets," she called out to passersby.

Breathing in the fragrance of her flowers she laughed happily. She was well pleased with herself. Today had been most profitable, even though it was early. Patting the pocket of her slightly threadbare apron, she smiled. London's tradesmen and wealthier merchants had opened up their shutters, displaying their wares. Beth had chosen a likely spot from which to sell her flowers. The nobs walked along here, those with a shilling or two to spare. Seth knew just how to bat her long thick lashes, how to flirt with the gents, enticing them to buy.

"Gillyflowers. Lavender. How about a fresh bouquet?" She held a bouquet toward a neatly dressed young man and brightly bedecked young woman hopefully.

"How much?" The bespectacled gentlemen paused in midstride. "How much for the lavender?"

"Tuppence!" Beth's wide blue eyes sparkled as she looked up at him but before she had time to make a sale, the woman, clinging to her gent's arm, tugged at his sleeve, sniffing her disdain.

"Come along, Arthur! Don't give even a pence to that ragged little beggar." She eyed Beth up and down as if she had suddenly grown two heads. "London sparrows! They should be forbidden to loiter in this part of the city."

"Beggar! Sparrow!" Beth's face flushed crimson at the insult. It wasn't true. She made an honest living the only way she knew how. "I earn my keep." She raised a defiant fist as the woman picked up her skirts and walked away, her gentleman safely in tow. Oh, how such haughty women angered her. Women who kept a careful distance away from her as they passed by as if fearful that contact with her person would soil their garments.

Peacocks, they thought themselves to be, but they were really only brightly feathered old hens.

Beth sighed, looking down at her own ragged garments. She wore a thin woolen dress of a faded blue that she had purchased secondhand on Petticoat Lane. Once the full-skirted garment had been fashionable, now it was sadly out of style. Over the dress she wore a white muslin apron with two large pockets in which she kept her coins. Beneath the skirt, that was far too short for her tall frame, peeked long, white woolen stockings and square-toed black shoes. Her attire was far from fashionable but it was the best she could do. There were times when she felt herself fortunate to keep food in her stomach and a roof over her head.

"But someday," she said to herself. Beth had not always been so poor. Once, before a financial disaster had brought her father low, he had been a prosperous cloth merchant. In those days, she had been dressed in silks and velvets, a miniature of the fashionable ladies of the "ton." She had been her father's pride and joy in those happy, tranquil days. His angel.

Clenching her hands into fists, she fought against her tears as the past hovered before her eyes. Beth's mother had died at her birth and her father had been lonely. But if only he hadn't married *that woman*. Why couldn't he have seen? Spending money was all that *she* cared about. Never about her new husband or her stepdaughter. She had goaded Beth's father into spending beyond his means, in making unwise decisions. Burdened under a mounting debt, Robert Longley had come under the influence of an unscrupulous money lender who had led him into ruin. The once proud merchant had been forced to go to the workhouse, losing every fiber of his self-respect.

"The workhouse!" Beth shuddered. The rules had been brutal. Married couples were not allowed to live together, thus her father's wife had fled from his side, later seeking a divorce. Only Beth had stayed with him, doing her best to keep his spirits up, though it was often difficult to keep her own mood cheerful. All meals were taken in silence. No one could leave the workhouse except to go to church or to school. It was like being in prison for all the freedom she had been granted. A terrible place that brought forth only nightmares. There was a great deal of inhumanity on the part of the overseers, even more so when her father had fallen ill.

"Somehow we'll get through this, Papa," she had insisted. "You'll get well. Things will be just like they were . . . you and I will get out of here." In truth, the only way her father had escaped was by dying a few months ago. An outbreak of fever at the workhouse had claimed him, though somehow Beth had survived.

A debtor was allowed no coffin, no name-stone. With this Beth bore the added grief of seeing her father buried in an unmarked grave, as if he had never even existed except in her memories. To them he had been as unimportant as the shovelful of dirt they flung on his body. Oh, how she had cursed them.

Heartbroken and alone, Beth had fled the workhouse to try to earn a living on her own. Times had been hard, but if life was not perfect, well, it was at least reasonably comfortable. She had food, a room she shared with three other girls in which to sleep, and the kinship of her friends. Above all, Beth was a survivor. Experience had taught her that she had to be.

"But someday . . ." Someday she would dress in velvets and lace again. She'd be just like one of those snobbish feathered and flowered young women she saw strutting around on the arms of handsome young gentlemen or riding in shiny black carriages.

Her eyes were drawn in the direction of a rotund man dressed in buff colored trousers, cambric shirt, a lustrous black frock coat, and pea green waistcoat. Beneath his pristine white collar was a shining black cravat decorated with a jeweled pin that glittered in the light as he moved. The most noticeable thing about him was his bald head, shining like an apple in the sunlight. From time to time he looked at his gold pocket watch. Beth took a step toward him. This one could afford several bouquets.

"Would you care to buy a flower, Sir?" She smiled, showing off her dimples, receiving an appreciative stare as his eyes swept from her head to her toes and back again.

"BiGod, I think I would!" Reaching into his waistcoat, he withdrew his moneypouch, a purse that bulged with coins. "Three bouquets if you take off that mobcap and let me see your pretty hair."

"Three bouquets?" It was even better than she had hoped. "Thank you, Sir." She reached in her basket for the flowers, catching sight of a tall faded hat out of the corner of her eye. The wearer bobbed in and out among the well-dressed patrons, coming toward Beth's gentleman customer.

Suddenly Beth guessed what the young man was about. He was going to steal from her generous gentleman. "He's a thief," she hissed beneath her breath. It was a thing she could never condone. No matter how poor one was it just wasn't right to steal. She might be poor but she had her ethics.

"The cap, girl. The cap. Let me see your hair."

"Hmmmmm?" She was distracted as she watched the man in the hat. He reminded her of a rakish-looking cat. Sleek. Graceful. Stealthfully, he descended with caution and slyness. Even so, she didn't want to "peech." He might be a thief, but she didn't want to see him put in prison. There had to be another way to avoid a robbery.

"Your cap, girl. It was part of the bargain. I want to see . . ."

Beth tugged at her mobcap as she inched her way forward, her eyes on the top-hatted young man. The young thief was quick. Before she could react or think of a way to stop the robbery the young man had slashed the strings of the gentleman's money pouch with a deft flick of his wrist. His eyes were sparkling with triumph, a grin cut its way from ear to ear as he turned in her direction. He didn't realize that he had been observed, but Beth did. A man dressed in black was watching the young man scrutinizingly. Now that man moved forward.

"Thief! Thief!" The cry rang through the air, spoken by more than one voice. Others had seen the young man's deed. "Catch him."

"Merry-go-up!" She watched him helplessly as a crowd of several blue-suited men closed in. Though she frowned upon stealing, Beth didn't want the pickpocket to be caught. Like her, he was a victim of his penury. She had heard about what happened behind the walls of Newgate. It was a fate she wouldn't have wished for even the most hardened criminal. Thinking that perhaps there was some way she might help him, she pressed closer. It was to be her undoing for, seeing her approach, the young man saw a chance of escaping his pursuers.

"Be a dear and taike care o' this," he whispered, pressing the stolen purse into her hands. He was off in a flash. Pushing into a bootblack, overturning the pieman's cart, and vaulting over it to safety, he vanished into the crowd.

"To the *Dial!*" she heard him say. He was heading to that haven of safety amidst the *rookeries* where seven streets intersected. If he made it there quickly he would lose his pursuers, as that area was a labyrinth of roads. Beth watched him flee, then looked down in confused perplexity at the purse in her hands. It seemed to burn like red hot coals and she jiggled it as if it burned her fingers. What to do with it?

"Sir . . ." She looked for its proper owner to promptly return it but he had joined with the young thief's pursuers. "Merry-go-up!" She likewise ran in that direction. Sir! Sir!"

A shrill voice rent the air. "That young woman has your purse, Sir!" A young chimney sweep added to the tumult of cries, pointing unflinchingly in Beth's direction. Like a tide, the throng of pursuers changed direction in mid-stride.

"The girl. She has my money pouch. She's a thief! A thief!" The gentleman's eyes blazed accusingly. "She targeted me for that young rogue's thievery."

"No, I . . . I didn't . . . I'm not . . ." It was no use. By his actions the young thief had set her up as his accomplice. With a cry of frustration she took to her heels. From the look of hostility on the faces around her, she'd get no mercy from anyone in the square.

With a fearful squeal of dismay, Beth took to her heels. Like hounds to a fox the men followed, screaming and shouting after her. The chase had begun in deadly earnest. Flitting across the road on legs made agile by desperation, Beth used her wits to avoid capture. The all-enveloping terror of being the prey pricked her. The urge for self-survival made her fleet of foot.

It seemed the chase went on for a long, long time. The following. The dodging. The satisfaction of losing them only to be found again. Changing direction several times, she confused her pursuers, plunging deeper and deeper into the alleys and courts and yards of that area known as the Dials. The threat of being caught goaded her on to run, run, run, even when she was too winded to go on. And yet, she heard the steady pounding of feet and knew the others had not given up pursuit. How much longer could she outdistance them?

The twisting streets of the Dial welcomed Beth like a well-known friend. Still she moved cautiously, stealing a quick glance up and down the tangle of merging roads. Damning the young thief with every breath, she thought how his impulsive action had nearly brought her to a sorry end. Anger boiled in her blood.

Beth looked around her. Her pursuers had vanished. She felt the elation of having outmaneuvered them yet, at the same time, she had a sinking feeling in her stomach. The number of people in the streets had thinned out and she found herself in a sorry part of town. Instinctively, she knew she should leave as quickly as she could before she got into further trouble. With that thought in mind she sauntered back the way she had come at a brisk pace.

Beth would have been hard put to say exactly when she became aware of the presence behind her. How long she had been followed she could not say. So, she had not escaped after all. Or was it a more devious hunter stalking her? She was overcome with sensations, an almost extraordinary sensitivity. It was as though she could see without looking, hear without listening, feel without touching. Every one of her senses screamed out at her. She was being followed by "one of them." She knew it.

"Above all, don't show fear!" she advised herself. The criminals in this area were like wild animals. They fed on fright. If she could manage to keep her calm, could seemingly blend in with this reeking slum, perhaps she might escape unharmed. After all, she was nearly as tattered as they.

Clutching the purse to her breast, she slipped into the shadows, marching on, never turning her head. She forced herself to hum a tune. If they thought she belonged they might not bother her. She tried to maintain her calm. All the while her feet struck the roadway with purposeful strides, carrying her out of the Dial. Better to face prison than a knife between her shoulder blades.

Beth moved toward the closest avenue of escape. Up ahead there was a space between two buildings, barely wide enough for two people to pass each other but seemingly the surest way out of the Dial. Taking a deep breath she started off in that direction. All would be well. She'd go back to her flat and have quite a story to tell Mary and Gilly. She willed herself to be brave but all her self-composure shivered into fragments as an iron-strong hand clasped her arm.

Two

"No! Leave me be!" The words came out in a sharp and breathy rush. Beth was a fighter. She wouldn't go down without a struggle. With all the courage she could muster she pulled free and hurled herself at her attacker.

Jamie braced his shoulders, knowing at once what the young woman had in mind, but even so the impact sent him hurling to the dirt. Then they were both sprawling, rolling over and over in the alley's filth, a tangle of arms and legs. "Wot in bloody 'ell?" The girl was much stronger than he might have thought. A feisty little scrapper.

The fall left Beth breathless. Winded. Even so, she flailed her arms and legs, catching Jamie with a sharp blow under the chin that forced his head back. He yelped out in pain and it was only then that Beth focused her eyes upon his face—handsome despite the grime their tussle had put there.

"You!" For just a moment she lay there panting. Staring. In suspended animation, she waited for him to make a move toward her again, but he didn't.

"I wasn't going ter harm yer," he said at last. "I just wanted ter talk wi' yer. No cause to hit me in the jaw." He rubbed that injured part with his long-fingered hand. "Yer pack quite a punch, yer do." In spite of his pain he grinned in a white flash of teeth, a disarming smile. He admired fortitude.

She sought to justify having struck out at him. "How was I to know what you intended? You would have done the same if I had crept up behind you."

"I don't think so, and yet again maybe I would 'ave."

They both lay still, trying to assess the situation, then, almost in unison, they both stood up. Beth tried to walk away but Jamie stopped her. He hadn't taken such a risk back there on the streets to come away empty-handed.

"The purse, Miss. I followed yer ter get wot was roightly mine, I did." He held out his hand.

"Yours?" Beth laughed sarcastically. "I know that to be an untruth. That purse didn't belong to you." Her mobcap had come loose in the struggle. The long auburn hair it had hidden tumbled like a cloak about her shoulders. Combing the tangled tresses, she tried to put some semblance of order to her wayward curls. "I know what you did. You took something that wasn't yours." Now that she knew he didn't have it in mind to hurt her in any way she made up her mind that he wouldn't get his ill-gotten gain so easily. She had to make him see that he had clearly been in the wrong.

"It was mine by roight of conquest." Why was it those huge blue eyes made him suddenly feel like such a cad? He'd never felt guilty before. "I . . . uh . . . confiscated it."

"Stole it!" Her perfectly arched brows drew together in a frown.

He threw his hands up in frustration. All roight, I *did* it." Her disdain wounded him and he hurriedly sought to justify his actions. "But from the looks o' 'im 'e didn't need it."

"That's beside the point. This purse belonged to him and you took it." Reaching down she picked up her cap, twisting it and turning it in her hands. "Stealing is wrong."

"Ha!" He squared his shoulders, though he averted his eyes. "I'd laiy yer odds that 'e cheated some poor bloke out o' those shillings and crowns. 'Ow else do yer think they get rich. Eh? Stealin' the same as me." He wrinkled his nose. "Only in a different waiy. I've seen that one before, I 'ave. Paiys his laborers such a low waige they 'ardly 'ave enough to feed their families. Robs from the poor, 'e does I. I only taikes from those wot can afford it."

"Even so, that doesn't make it right." Beth's voice was strong as she voiced her conviction. "Besides, that's not the worst of it." Crossing her arms in front of her chest her blue eyes sparked fire. "You set me up." The memory of that horrible moment flashed before her eyes and she felt a renewal of anger. "Coward! Blighter!" Her voice was so loud in accusation that it was nearly a shout. "I could have gone to Newgate because of what you did."

For that he was truly repentant. He would never have wanted that. "Reflex action, it was. Self-preservation. I didn't stop to think wot might 'ave 'appened if yer got caught. I'm sorry." He'd been cornered after all.

"You're sorry!" The more she thought about it the angrier she was.

"Gore, but I don't know why yer got yer back up." He clucked his tongue. "Yer outran the blighters."

"I did. But even though I got away I'm ruined. The best corner in all of London and it will be forbidden to me now. I won't be able to stake out that spot for fear of being fingered by that gentleman you stole from. He'll have me sent to prison as a thief."

"Find other digs . . ."

She snapped her fingers. "Just like that. I had good luck selling flowers there." What was the use? Alleycat that he was he just didn't understand. They had a far different set of values. She shook her head. "You come into my life like a thunderstorm, make me an accomplice to your stealing, and then say . . ."

"I said that I was sorry, and I am." His voice was soft, husky. He leaned forward and looked down at her, admiring her long, slim neck, the pretty oval face so close to his own. Her facial features intrigued him. Her profile was as perfect as a cameo's. He wondered what she would do were he to brush her lips in a kiss, but seeing the ferocity in her expression decided she would most likely slap him. Some other time then. He did, however, touch her face to brush away a smudge of dirt on her chin. Her skin was soft. Smooth.

"How easy it is to say. You're sorry . . ." Beth swallowed nervously as she felt his fingers lightly stroke her face. Lifting her head, she found her face so close to his that one of the curls at his temple stirred as he breathed. As he moved forward she felt her breasts lightly press against his chest. A wave swept over her, replacing her rage with a far different emotion. A quiver of awareness danced up and down her spine. Every instinct within her was abruptly awakened. Oh, he was dangerous all right, but not in the way she had first supposed.

"Please . . ." She found herself looking directly at the chiseled strength of his lips and wondered what they would feel like—firm or soft. What would it be like to kiss him. She jerked away as if he had burned her.

His voice was a soft, deep rumble. "Please? Please wot?"

Fighting to calm the rapid beating of her heart she took a deep breath. "Please, take the purse and let me be." She swallowed again, torn between wanting to stay and wanting to flee.

"Ah, yes. The purse." He grinned as he remembered what had brought them together in the first place. "If yer intend ter give it to me then I suppose yer 'ave at least a bit of forgiveness in your 'eart for me? I don't believe that yer are still angry."

She thrust the money pouch into his hands. As she did so their fingers touched in a caress. Staring at her hand, Beth tried not to think of the gentleness those strong fingers had expressed. "I am . . . but . . . but . . ." She didn't want to argue. What else was there but to give the purloined money pouch to him. To seek out the true owner would be an awkward situation. How could she ever make him believe what had really happened?

He winked. "But nevertheless yer loike ole Jamie."

She did and was horrified that it showed. "It . . . It's late. I . . . I have to go."

"Late? The sun is as bright in the sky as ever. It's early."

"I want to go." If she stayed here a minute longer something was going to happen between her and this man. The very air crackled with anticipation. She didn't want that. A man who preyed on other men and women could never win her heart. And yet, dear God how his very nearness drew her.

Jamie was a man who knew women well and he sensed her attraction to him. He also perceived her innocence, her nervousness. Any other time he might have taken advantage of the situation, of a lovely girl so vulnerable to an embrace, but strangely he didn't this time. Somehow, despite her spunk, her spirit, he sensed her to be as soft and delicate as the flowers she sold.

"By all means, go!" He wanted to keep her here just a little while longer but he didn't allow his thoughts to show. He tried to tell himself that she just wasn't his type, that he preferred women with more experience, but it was a lie. Still, there was little purpose in seducing her. Let this one keep her naivete a bit longer. He knew he had a way with women. He wouldn't be pining for her very long. With a rakish grin he tipped his hat. "I'd be willin' ter share my spoils wi' yer before yer do, 'owever."

"No!" Beth caught her breath, holding it for an instant before she could gain control of her voice again. "I wouldn't feel right."

"A pity." From the looks of her she was nearly as poverty-stricken as he. More so. He really would have liked to give her part of his bounty, but he didn't push the matter. Everyone had to follow his own conscience. "Well then, I suppose it's time to go our separate waiys."

"It is time." Even so, she hesitated. There were so many things she might have said, but didn't. Questions to ask. She didn't even know his name. She might have asked him but just then the solitude of the alleyway was intruded upon as a giggling quartet of drunken revelers pushed through a doorway. Beth and Jamie were no longer alone. It was as if the spell was broken. Thus the questions went unasked.

Beth walked a few steps, then turned for one last look. The chance that she would ever see him again was very slim. London was crowded to the brim with people. Perhaps it was for the best. "Goodbye." There was nothing more that she could say.

Three

The Dial was an irregular square into which streets and courts plunged in all directions. Seven to be exact. A thief or miscreant could get lost, vanishing into the unwholesome vapor that enveloped the city, a blend of fog and smoke. It was near the Dial that the tenement Jamie shared with several other pickpockets was located. Odd how the stench of the narrow cobbled street assailed Jamie's nostrils more noticeably today as he hurried back to the place he flippantly called "home." Why was that? Because of that blue-eyed girl?

"Mmmmm . . ."

He remembered how she had smelled, so clean and fresh, like lavender soap mixed with violets. And her face, so pretty and wide-eyed. For just a moment he smiled as he remembered. Whoever she was, she was the kind of young woman a man imagined with children tugging at her skirts. A respectable type. The type of woman that made a gent want to settle down and . . .

"Blimey," he whispered, "but she maikes me think dangerous thoughts." Thoughts that he had no business thinking. He was what he was and he intended to be happy with what he was. He had food, the warmth of a fire, and the friendship of the other "vagabonds" that shared the dwelling behind the pawnbroker's shop in Orley Square. What's more, he was the favorite of Annie, the leader of the group and thus was more often than not shown favoritism.

Annie Kingsley had a network of contacts to insure her own safety, unscrupulous parish beadles, prison turnkeys, greedy magistrates, and here and there a bobby who would turn his head. In return, she gave them cash, liquor, or favors in some form or other. Not bribery, but trading justices, she called it, as did many others in her profession. She was important and the way she treated Jamie made him feel important as well.

For the moment he was content, or at least he told himself he should be. Why then, as he briefly closed his eyes, did he conjure up those wide, innocent, pale blue eyes? Why did he find himself wishing . . .

Jamie passed by the secondhand clothing store, two gin shops, and several assorted broken-down dwellings, many with rags or papers in the broken windows, familiar sights and part of his habitat. Usually the broken-down buildings went unnoticed as he sauntered by, but today they seemed to jump out at him. Oh, what a stark contrast this was to the "other" side of town where men rode in fine carriages and wore smartly tailored suits.

Somedaiy I'll dress loike that and ride about town all in style. I will." Someday . . .

In the meantime, Jamie was resolved to accept his surroundings and above all to keep Annie happy. As long as he pleasured her and soothed her with his smiles he would make out just fine.

"G'daiy, Jamie . . ." A tall, grinning patched and tattered man greeted Jamie as he turned the corner, tipping his hat in the manner he'd seen gentlemen affect.

"G'daiy, Gideon."

"Were the pickin's good?"

Jamie shrugged. "Fair to middlin'. Just fair to middlin'." With a smile he secretively clutched the money pouch. "Where's Annie?"

"Upstairs." He poked his thumb in that direction.

"Is that so . . ." Laughing softly, Jamie took the stairs two at a time, giving the plump and pretty woman a soft pat on the behind as he opened the door. " 'Ere I am love, in case yer been lookin' fer me."

This time, however, Annie seemed not in the mood for lovemaking. Though she smiled and eyed her handsome "consort" up and down she got right to business. "Any shillings for me, Jamie dearie?" The blonde woman blocked his way as she held out her hand.

He was playful. "Maiybe there is and then again maiybe no, but a kiss might just open me lips." He closed the door.

She moved into his arms with the grace of a sensuous cat but before they had time for even a kiss a loud pounding interrupted their passionate solitude. With a curse, Annie exited, talking angrily to the intruder.

Jamie put his ear to the door, furling his brow as he heard bits and pieces. Woe his bad luck and ill-timing. An informant was telling Annie that the gentleman whose purse Jamie had pinched was a magistrate of some importance who had unfortunately gotten enough of a look at the young rogue to give out a description. A price had been put on Jamie's head. Worse yet, his act of bravado might well endanger Annie's entire operation were his whereabouts to be found out.

"Ye fool! Yer cocky, swaggering fool!" Picking up an empty gin bottle, Annie heaved it at his head. "Ye will ruin us all!"

Jamie ducked just in time to avoid being clobbered. "Now, now, Annie." Though her words were only too true, Jamie sought to placate her. He couldn't chance being turned out on the street. Not now! "I'll think o' somethin'."

Her eyes narrowed. "Well, yer better think of *somethin'* quickly, me boy. "I haven't worked all these years ter up my surroundings only to be ruined, even if it is by the loikes o' a devilishly handsome bloke."

Jamie grinned, feeling safe and secure despite the circumstances. Despite her anger Annie wouldn't throw him to the wolves. "I'll change me line of work, love, for the time being. I'll be as they say, 'nocturnal.' "

Annie wrinkled her brow, still he could tell that she was thinking the matter over favorably. "Aye. it might bloody well work. Yer could sleep during the day and work at night."

"Aye. I'll sleep during the mornings and that waiy we'll 'ave the afternoons to plaiy." Jamie winked.

Annie folded her arms, scrutinizing him. "Now, let's see. Just what could we 'ave yer do?"

Each of Annie's people had a specialty to come up with his weekly allotment of goods or money. There were all sorts of professions represented here—thieves, swindlers, robbers, and smugglers.

Dirk was a rat catcher, sent aboard cargo ships to get rid of the destructive vermin. Little did the ships' captains know that he carried the same live rats from vessel to vessel creating the opportunity to steal as he went. Three of the women and two of the children were *mudlarks*, or scuffle hunters as some called them. They would wade in water, lurking in silt beneath moored ships to catch the packages thrown to them from those aboard who were in cahoots. Pete pretended to be blind, robbing his unsuspecting victims when they were unaware. Eve used her beauty to lure men, then robbed the poor blokes blind.

"Ow abouts I do wot Freddie does?" His lay was stealing luggage by cutting the ropes which bound traveling chests to carriages. Or then again there was Paddy, whose specialty was waiting in inn yards, offering his service to carry baggage, then stealing it.

"Mmmmmm . . . 'ow about yer being a mudlark?"

Jamie couldn't tell if Annie was serious or teasing. "A mudlark?" Quickly he shook his head. It was a task far beneath him, one which required that he be up to his chest in water and mud. "Not fer me!"

As a matter of fact, the more Jamie thought about it the more he determined that none of the other jobs suited him. Still, even he was surprised when a suggestion passed his lips.

"I want to learn to be a gentleman. Aye, that's it. Learn to talk and act loike the swells." He paused only long enough to quiet Annie's boisterous laugh. "I'm serious."

Jamie was reflective. "Wot separates gentlemen from men like me," he said aloud. "Money of course. Manners. A proper waiy of speaking. And luck." Plopping down into a well-padded chair he leaned back. "And of course, it doesn't 'urt to 'ave a rich wife."

Suddenly he found himself entertaining a preposterous idea, namely to learn to talk like those gentlemen did. He could masquerade as one of the "swells" and marry himself a fine, rich lady, sharing the spoils with Annie, of course."

"A gentleman . . . Marry a rich woman . . ." Annie came up behind him and ran her fingers through his hair. "I would scoff at such an idea were it anyone but you, Jamie."

Now it was Annie who allowed herself to dream. She envisioned herself being set up as his mistress in a fine house with servants, and all the chocolates she could eat. She could wear silks and velvets and pearls.

"Yer see!" Eagerly, Jamie verbally ticked off all his wishes and desires. He'd have a fine carriage, a gold watch fob, a diamond stick pin. All he needed was a chance, a chance which Annie now agreed to give him.

"Ye'll 'ave ter learn 'ow to pronounce yer words, how to walk, how ter bow.' With that thought in mind she stealthfully retrieved the hidden stash of valuables in the mattress of her bed. Her treasure would be used to finance Jamie's "education."

The large tenement room was dirty, ill-proportioned, and in a shambles from disrepair. Plaster peeled in strips from the walls, windows were broken and stuffed with rags. Straw mattresses lined the walls with not even a partition between them. Clearly, privacy was at a premium here. The women slept on one side of the room, the men on the other, but it was not unusual to hear sounds in the night that told very plainly what was going on. Indeed, Beth had been accosted in such a manner a number of times until she learned how to defend herself. Now she was a scrapper, known to have the claws of a lion and to pack quite a punch.

Beth sighed. Oh, how she longed to better herself. With that hope in mind she had been saving her shillings. Someday she would get out of here and return to the life she had once known. Little did she care that more often than not she was the butt of her friends' joking and laughter. She could almost hear them now.

"Bethie 'ere thinks she's going ter be a laidy," they had teased whenever she even proposed such an idea.

"Queen of the flower sellers, 'ats our Elizabeth."

"Oh, she'll saive enough all roigt, by the time she is eighty."

"If she lives that long, that is."

Smoke filled the room like fog. In the corner stood a wood-burning stove with an iron frying pan atop one of the burners. The appetizing smell of frying bacon scraps and cheese mingled with the aroma of onions. A trestle table in the middle of the room held a single candle that lit the gloom of the interior. Cracked plates, cups, and several burned out candle stubs littered the planked wooden table top. Several of the tenants had already gathered around the table, anxious to get their share of food.

"I will get out of here, I will!" Beth was determined. She would work morning and night if she had to. She'd sell twice as many flowers. She'd take a night time job she'd . . .

"Sit down, Beth. Hurry, or there won't be any food left."

Another flower-seller named Ruth, tugged at her sleeve. Protectively, she grabbed for a plate, put it down in front of Beth and dished up a portion of the food.

"There." With a smile she said, "pretend that it is the finest beef in all the land."

"Pretend." Beth sighed, wishing she could envision things the way Ruth did. It was almost as if Ruth could actually see things the others could not even imagine. Even though she was lame in one leg and had to use crutches she never complained. She saw flowers where there were only rags and refuse. Stardust where there was only dirt and grime. Diamonds where there were only tears and raindrops.

Beth looked around her, trying to see the room through Ruth's eyes. The floor was strewn with all manner of debris—heaps of rags, old jackets, and shawls and coats which made up the beds.

The walls were dirty and cracked, the ceiling had a lopsided appearance due to a water drip from above which had permeated the wood. The stairs leading to the room were old and rickety. In truth, it was merely a place to sleep and eat, hardly fit for living quarters, certainly not a real home. And yet to Ruth it had become special. Ruth was the only one who didn't laugh at Beth's yearning to better her circumstances.

"How much did yer get toiday?"

Beth's expression told the tale.

"Not much?"

"No." Her encounter with that bold young thief had distracted her so severely that she had been unable to even think, much less sell flowers. "I'll be here forever." It was a disturbing and troubling thought.

"Perhaps not!"

Beth took a bite of her porridge and shuddered, longing for the taste of meat. "I will. Barley is right. It will take me the next sixty years to make enough money to buy my own house. I'll never get out of here."

"You will!" Staunchly, Ruth defended Beth's dream, eagerly telling her about the woman that she had met that day. " 'Er name is Catherine Claremont. She is a lonély woman, she is. So lonely." Nearly as lonely as Beth, her expression seemed to say. "She is looking for a maid."

"A maid?" Beth cocked her head. "Perhaps I could clean her house and make more money."

"Or perhaps yer could live with the poor woman and give her the companionship that she wants."

Ruth's enthusiasm was contagious as she explained her conversation with the woman. She wanted someone to cook and to clean, someone who was good at lively conversation, someone who could make her smile.

"That's you, Beth. I told her so."

"Told her?"

"Aye" Happily, Ruth confided that she had taken it upon herself to set up an interview with Catherine Claremont for Beth.

"An interview?" Beth's hands shook as she held her spoon. "When?"

"Tomorrow morning. First thing."

It was a dark and moonless night. A sudden wind chilled Jamie's body as he looked over his shoulder, carefully making certain that no one was following him. It seemed safe enough, so he proceeded.

The streets were swarming with hackney coaches and carriages that were transporting splendidly dressed men and women to various destinations—theatres, taverns, cozily lighted inns, or perhaps to more intimate rendezvous. The *nobs,* Jamie thought, and among such as these he was to find a likely *pigeon.*

"One last job. Then I'll be finished wi' thievery," he thought to himself.

Tonight, because of Annie's nagging, he would follow Freddie's example and steal a bit of luggage, hoping that it would be profitable enough to finance his new life as a gentleman. Ah, but tonight would be the last time he would soil his hands stealing.

"One last job . . ."

Hiding in the shadows, Jamie stared assessingly at the throng of people who rode and walked about the cobbled streets. There had to be someone here who was a likely mark. He needed to pick an inn-yard out and be quick about it. But which one? There were several.

One inn, The Boar's Head, caught his eye, an old-fashioned three-story, whitewashed building with boxed windows that looked over the Thames. It was the one inn that seemed to be exhibiting a popularity for frock-coated and top-hatted men. Better yet, the outer courtyard did not seem to be as busy as the others, therefore making it a safer place to ply his trade.

Walking stealthfully across the street he took notice of his surroundings. Noise emanated from within the inn's taproom, drunken laughter, singing, boisterous carrying on told him the inn's patrons would be distracted. They were busy inside "making merry" and would be less likely to interfere in what he had planned. Ah, yes, there would be far less chance of being caught in such a place.

Opening the inn's creaking door he scanned his surroundings. It was murky inside with the smell of stale wine and ale mixed with the "gentlemen's" perfume. Wisely, Jamie had changed his garments before setting out for the inn. He wore a coat of olive-green, brown trousers, and brown boots so that he would look the part of a gentleman himself, for it was not his purpose to attract undue attention. He did in fact blend in well with the chattering crowd.

One man stood out, however—an extremely unpleasant character who had just barely escaped the hangman's noose. Howie Townsend was a thief, a swindler and worst of all, a murderer. For much less than a shilling he would slit any man's throat.

"I wonder wot on earth 'e's doing here?" The thief's presence boded no good. Still, Jamie was anxious to finish what he had started so that he could put this all behind him.

Hurrying to the inn-yard he dodged in and out among the carriages, blending with the night as he examined each one. Five of the carriages had no luggage at all, clearly showing that their patrons were staying the night and had therefore taken their baggage inside. Ah, but one carriage was heaped high to the sky with leather boxes, bags, and reticules. There was only one problem. It was also being guarded by a brawny brute that looked as if he could put up quite a fight.

"Hmmmmm . . ." Always a man to avoid violence if he could, Jamie thought of creating a diversion. Fumbling about for a large rock, Jamie grabbed one, took aim, and hurled it toward the inn's rooftop several feet away.

The brawny man turned his head, but unfortunately didn't budge.

Jamie picked up another rock, and threw it toward the same target. When the man still didn't move, he repeated his actions again and again. At last he was rewarded.

"Who's there?" Stumbling through the darkness, the brawny man headed in the opposite direction of the sound.

"Brilliant, Jamie ole boy. Brilliant!"

Jamie was quick to congratulate himself. Pulling a small knife from his pocket he quickly went to work sawing through the thick ropes that held the trunks atop the carriage, imagining all the while the valuable things he would find inside. Fine linen or silk shirts, perhaps, with pearl or silver buttons. Fine hats and gloves. Or if the owner was a married man accompanied by his wife, perhaps a velvet dress or two. They could be sold at either Petticoat Lane or at the rag fair in Rosemary Lane for a profitable price. And if he were lucky, there might even be something more valuable inside, like a watch, a wallet, or money pouch hidden.

"Agh . . ." Jamie grunted as he lifted the heavy leather suitcase down from its perch. Should he take it and run? Perhaps. And yet the other, smaller bag teased him, tempted him. He reached up.

"You there! What the bloody hell are you about?"

Gasping in dismay at having been caught, Jamie thought quickly. "Why I be for the inn, Sir. I was just 'elping yer by taking the luggage in, I was!"

"A likely story!"

Jamie squared his shoulder and feigned innocence. "I was!"

"You're a thief! I know all about what you do. That's why I was standing here, to thwart the likes of you."

"Me?"

"Yes, you!" Effortlessly he pushed Jamie against a brick wall, cutting off any avenue of escape. "The bobbies will be interested in nabbing you."

The very threat made Jamie feel as if he were choking. "Please, Sir. I didn't mean any 'arm, I didn't." All Jamie wanted at that moment was to be away from here.

"Don't plead for yourself. I know your game. Well, we'll see what the law has to say. We'll . . ." With a groan he suddenly slumped forward, his lips forming an endless grimace of agony.

Puzzled, Jamie stared at him and in that moment understood

what had happened. Right behind the man stood Howie Townsend, a knife in his hand. The blade had pierced the other man's back.

"Ye've killed him, yer 'ave!" Jamie's eyes were accusing as he bent his head to listen for a heartbeat. He heard a strong ticking. The man was alive.

"If I 'aven't I'll bloody well will now. 'E sent my brother to Newgaite. 'E deserves it." He wielded the knife with deadly intent as he crouched down.

"No!" Stealing was one thing, murder another. Jamie would have none of it, nor could he stand by and see it done. Throwing himself in the way of Townsend's knife he exhibited a show of daring and bravery that surprised and unnerved the assailant.

"Get out o' the waiy or ye'll get the saime thing!" He brandished the knife threateningly, used to everyone cowering.

"Noooooo! I won't go. And wot's more if ye 'arm 'im I'll let out a cry that will bring down the 'ouse, I will." Clenching his jaw Jamie held his ground, determined to do everything necessary to keep the dark-haired thief from carrying out his intent. "Awaiy wi' yer now."

"Argh . . . Vexed, Townsend threw up his hands, not out of fear of Jamie but because he realized that several eyes were looking their way. Taking to his heels the thief fled, merging into the same darkness that had spawned him.

Again Jamie knelt beside the wounded man staring down at his face. "I'll get yer some 'elp, I will."

The man didn't answer, nor did he even move—not an eyelid, not a finger, not a muscle. He was out cold. Or *was* he dead?

"What has happened here?" The voice shattered Jamie's already taut nerves.

" 'E's been stabbed!"

"You mean that you've killed him."

"No! Not I!"

Every instinct screamed at Jamie that he had to get away. Quickly. No one would believe him. No one! Nor would it be the first time a bystander was arrested for such a deed. In the uproar for vengeance there could be a hanging first and questions asked afterward. Was it any wonder the common man's view of justice was so cynical?

"Then who?" The expression in the man's eyes clearly showed that he marked Jamie guilty.

Jamie didn't wait to say another word. Pushing past the man he ran toward the bushes, putting as much distance as he could from himself and the inn.

"Follow him! Don't let him get away." The sound of shouting and the trampling of feet told him clearly that he was still in danger. Picking himself up from the ground, he used the night as a cloak to stealthfully make his escape.

The square courtyard of the inn was the scene of total pandemonium. The night's events had drawn a curious crowd who hovered about like moths to a flame, chattering their questions.

It was no wonder that fear goaded Jamie to run and run until he was exhausted. A wave of sickness washed over him as he thought about what nearly happened. He had witnessed a stabbing. It little mattered that in actuality he had been a hero. No one would believe him. He would be hunted down unmercifully. Unless . . .

He had to get away! The words pounded in his head, pushing him to run as fast as his legs would carry him. The sound of running feet and curses was carried to his ears by the wind. Worse yet, soon every doorway and gateway was blocked to his escape. Where could he hide? Where would he be safe from detection?

Indecision fueled his frustration until his eyes lit upon a carriage at the upper end of the street. The horses were harnessed and ready for travel. In all probability the carriage would soon be wheeling its way up the street toward some unknown destination.

"A carriage." How convenient!" Stumbling through the darkness, Jamie darted in and out between crates and barrels as he made his way toward the intended hiding place. Upon reaching the carriage he crawled underneath, clinging to the axel. Feeling relieved that there was no sound of pursuit he smiled, then moved his lips in a silent prayer, a prayer that was seemingly answered as the minutes passed by in silence.

The sound of footsteps disturbed the quietude. From his hiding place Jamie could see the hem of a skirt and shoes, dainty white satin slippers. "Here you go, Mrs. Claremont!"

"Mrs. Claremont," he whispered beneath his breath. The name of his rescuer. Closing his eyes, he tried for a moment to envision her appearance. No doubt she was plain faced and spoiled. The rich usually were. Even so, he made a mental point of it to find out for himself.

Jamie held his breath in anticipation, exhaling in relief as he felt the floorboards jiggle and sway as the woman stepped into the carriage, settling herself on the front seat. Soon the carriage was bouncing and creaking as it moved down the road.

Four

Through the tiny window of the room she shared with Ruth, Beth could hear the sounds of London—the clatter of the carts, the barking of the hounds, the din of pedestrians as they wound their way past shops, the voices of peddlers hustling their wares. Smokestacks from factories, church spires, and steeply pitched roofs rose in a hotchpotch against the hazy skies of the city. A dark cloud hung over Soho as smoke from the hundreds and hundreds of chimneys, forges, and furnaces mingled in a thick fog. It could be suffocating in this part of town. Clouds of sulphur, full of stink and darkness often left a man's suit or a woman's dress covered with soot, but today promised to be a bright sunny day, so Beth ignored the smoke as she rose from the bed and leaned over the sill.

"I think you are right, Ruth. I think perhaps today might just be the day that could bring the fulfillment of my dreams."

That was the opinion she held as she strolled through Petticoat Lane, Rosemary Lane, Holywell Street, and Monmouth Street.

Beth had discarded her mobcap and the loose fitting dress for something more stylish—an imitation of the ladies of quality she saw walking daintily along the streets. She owned two dresses, which she alternated as the mood suited her. Today she wore the blue linen with puffed sleeves, filled in with a tucker to hide the low neckline. If it was patched and torn in a few places, well, it was still fashionable. As for hats, she had chosen one with a rigid brim which held her auburn curls tightly to frame her face.

Beth was sure of herself, that is until she reached the address Ruth had given her. The sight of the two carved lions, lions that looked so real they nearly threatened to eat her, the huge door, the sculpted hedges, and the all-imposing air of grandeur made her feel horribly out of place. Perhaps she did belong exactly where she was. How foolish she was to dream.

"Yes?" The small, piercing eyes that looked at her as the butler opened the door unnerved her. Likewise, the hazel eyes of Catherine Claremont seemed to stare into her very soul.

Biting her lip nervously, Beth said softly, "I've come for the interview. To . . . to be your companion." For just a moment she felt primed and ready to flee.

"You are Elizabeth?" The tall woman with snow white hair but a face remarkably young for her age looked Beth up and down.

"I am, Mistress Claremont." Beth smiled shyly. "But I wish that you would call me Beth." She curtsied politely.

"Indeed. Beth." The woman's eyes held a sudden kindness. "I like it. And you of course must call me Catherine. Otherwise I just might feel like your grandmother and I want to feel young, you see."

"You are young!"

"In my heart I fear, but not in my body." For a moment the woman looked very sad. "You can buy most things you see, but no one has found a way to give us back our youth. A youth which is wasted on the young." She paused a moment then freely gave a compliment. "You are a very pretty young woman. Yes, you are. And sweet as well. I think that you will do quite nicely."

The butler started to whisper something in her ear but Catherine Claremont nudged him in the ribs. "Come in and sit down, child. You fascinate me."

Leading her into the drawing room, Catherine Claremont motioned toward a chair, saying simply, "Sit. Tell me all about yourself."

Beth did, strangely opening up to this woman she didn't even know. By the end of the monologue she felt a sense of peace. It was good to talk about the past with someone who didn't heap scorn upon her head. "And someday I want to be a lady."

"A lady?" The butler looked down his nose at her, instigating Beth's anger.

Stiffening her back and raising her chin, Beth glared up at the servant. "Yes a lady! And I'm going to, too! No one is going to keep me down!"

"Bravo!" Catherine Claremont clapped her hands. "I admire your spunk, Beth. You do in fact remind me of myself once. I too struggled to make my way in life after fate had given me much heartache"

"You struggled."

"I did." She smiled. "Oh yes, you will most certainly, too. I like you. Moreover, you have a certain grace in the way you hold yourself, a loveliness that even, uh . . . circumstances have not been able to steal away. In another setting this auburn-haired girl could well be a jewel."

"You mean . . ." Everything was going so well that she wanted to pinch herself to make certain it wasn't all a dream.

"Of course. I want you to live with me, Beth." She smiled apologetically. "Of course that will mean that you will be expected to do some work."

Beth nodded enthusiastically. "I will. I will."

"But for the most part we will be friends, you and I. Would you like that?"

Beth said she would, staring wide-eyed as she was shown the imposing interior of the mansion. It wasn't so much the elegance of her new surroundings, however, as much as it was the warmth she suddenly felt. Strangely enough, although she had never met this woman before, had never been inside the house until this day, she felt at home.

Stretching his cramped arms and legs, Jamie yawned. Oh, but he ached in every joint. It was such a hard bed. He'd have to tell

Annie to get a softer mattress, one that was filled with goose feathers instead of . . .

"Annie . . ." He reached out for her, his hand striking cold metal. A door handle. "Wot!" He opened his eyes, realizing that he wasn't in his room. Then where was he?

Lifting his head, he peered cautiously out the oblong window of the shiny black carriage. Now he remembered. Last night he had hidden beneath this carriage, somehow managing to hang on until it had reached its destination.

Jamie was exhausted and lulled by the rocking of the carriage as it moved along the bumpy roadway toward London. Closing his eyes he wondered about the woman's appearance. Would Catherine Claremont have the face of an angel or would she be as ugly as a hag?

Cautiously, he had waited until the owner of the carriage was safely inside her house and he was alone. Then and only then had he been brave enough to open the door and fling himself inside, feeling bruised and a bit battered.

"Well, I've slept in stranger places," he whispered, leaning his head against the padded leather seat.

In all actuality, it was surprisingly comfortable inside the carriage. Jamie had whiled away the time by looking around him. The sides were panelled, the semicircular top covered with characteristic ornamentation both inside and out. The windows on the door had curtains that could be drawn to give a small measure of privacy. For the moment he felt safe.

"Catherine Claremont," he exclaimed, remembering the name. He grinned as he wondered what she would think if she knew of her having saved his skin last night. No doubt she would turn her haughty little nose up in horror. To the nobs he was just a street rat, a non-entity, a nothing. Ah, but one of these days he would come back here wearing his fancy clothes and then it would be a far different matter.

"I'll give 'er one of me smiles and she'll be eatin' out of me 'and!" He felt smug. Now that the fear of last night had evaporated with the morning sun he felt more sure of himself as his old bravado returned.

The complacent security he felt was soon threatened, however. The sound of footsteps warned Jamie of danger. Someone was coming. Fearing discovery he pushed the carriage door open and once again took to the streets.

Jamie wandered around the foggy streets of London like a lost soul, not knowing quite what to do with himself. Over and over again he remembered all that had happened. "By God, if only he hadn't tried to steal that baggage. Ah, but he had. Now all he could hope was that no one had gotten too good a look at him. It might well ruin his plans.

"No!" He wouldn't allow anything to do that. He'd grow a mustache and trim his hair a different way, that would help to disguise him. He'd hurry and learn how to change his pattern of speech, that too would aid him in his masquerade.

The fog was much thicker now, like wisps of smoke curling around him as he walked. Annie would be furious with him for coming away empty-handed. Worse yet, it would give her the upper hand if she used her money to finance his trek into gentlemanhood. And yet, now he had no other choice. As soon as he could he'd pay her back in full so that he could have his freedom.

"Freedom, ha!" Reaching into his pocket he was dismayed to find that he had only the price of a drink. It would take him a long, long time to attain his dream. Though Jamie drank sparingly he found himself seeking out Weasel's Tavern. There he would try to drown his sorrow in gin as he hid away from the dangers of the outside world.

It was musky and smoky inside this hell hole. The stink of whiskey and ale hung in the air, mingling with the odor of sweat and leather, a sad comparison to the inn's taproom he had visited last night. Ah, but one day . . .

Ordering a gin, the poor man's drink, Jamie stared into the depths of his cup as if perchance to glimpse the future. One day he'd be drinking the finest whiskey. Holding the glass to his lips he let some of the potent liquid trickle down his throat.

Five

Catherine Claremont's keen eyes softened as she looked at her new companion. The young woman waited so eagerly, clutching so tightly to her lone suitcase, that she was deeply touched. For just a moment Beth looked like a child.

"Come in, my dear. From now on my home will be your home. I want you to feel comfortable here." Strange, Catherine thought, how she could look so lovely even in those sadly out of fashion clothes.

Catherine hoped most sincerely that the warmth of her kindness might revive the girl's tender beauty and the spirit that lay beneath her nervousness. Beth had already revealed an enormous amount of aptitude, surprising the old woman with the fact that she could read, write, and do her sums. Those were not skills she had learned from the inhabitants of Rosemary Lane, she thought. Somewhere in the girl's background was a respectable heritage.

"Good afternoon, Missus . . ." Beth then corrected herself, "Catherine."

"Good afternoon." And it was a good one. Now for the first time she felt the hope of enjoying life again, seeing all the things she'd become so accustomed to and taken for granted, through this young woman's eyes. It was, by proxy, a return to her youth.

The house was enormous and beautifully decorated with chandeliers, wooden paneling, diamond shaped panes of glass in the windows, and flights and flights of stairs, all fully carpeted. Beth remembered how, when she was first told it was to be her home, she had wandered through each room, admiring the furniture, running her hands over the smooth velvets and intricately carved wood. Claremont House had twenty rooms including a library with a vast supply of leather bound books. Someday when she had the time she was going to read every one!

The front lawns stretched out on both sides of a cobbled drive, artfully landscaped with a checkerboard of flowerbeds and shrubbery. There was a small, separate house for the servants, a livery stable, a carriage house, a gazebo, a guest house, a gardener's shed. Houses for everything in fact. So many outbuildings that it was difficult for Beth to come to terms with such wealth when there was so much poverty in London. It made her feel somewhat guilty at times, remembering that while she slept on a soft bed there were those who had no bed at all.

"Ruthie . . ."

"What dear?"

"Nothing." Beth was wistful, suddenly missing Ruth with all of her heart. Oh, how she wished the young woman was here to talk to.

"I'll have Mollie fix us a spot of tea. I believe the cook has baked some crumpets, would you like some?"

Beth's face brightened. "Oh, yes!" She always adored the small unsweetened bread, gently cooked on a griddle then split and toasted. She moves so gracefully, Catherine thought. Dressed in the right clothes she would dazzle London society. Oh yes, she was like a little bud, just waiting to be nurtured so that she could come to full flower.

Catherine led the way toward the settee. "Come, let's talk awhile. Randolph can take your bag up to your room." They settled themselves by the window, exchanging pleasantries and just getting to know each other.

Soon the days settled into an established routine. Breakfast was precisely at seven, for Catherine Claremont would not abide loitering in bed all morning. Then Beth would busy herself with light household chores. Lunch was always an elaborate affair. Beth's once lithe figure had acquired voluptuous curves, though she feared that if she didn't have more willpower with sweet-meats, she'd soon be rotund.

The afternoon was spent with Beth reading to her companion. Finding out how skilled Beth was at numbers, Catherine had enlisted her aid in keeping financial records. One name had a ledger all its own. Ned Pritchart. Upon asking the old woman just who that was, she was met with a scowl

"My good for nothing nephew, that's who he is. A wastrel, a scoundrel. I fear you'll meet him soon enough."

"Ned?"

"Ned." Quickly, Catherine changed the subject. "But let us talk no more about him. I want to talk about you. About your wishes, your dreams." The woman paused. "Are there any young men in your life?"

Beth shook her head. "No."

Catherine smiled. "Well, we will have to change that, for there should be." With that thought in mind she set upon a course of action to turn Beth into a living doll, a fashion plate. She did in fact treat Beth much more like the daughter she had never had than as a hired companion.

Catherine had introduced Beth to the "finest" music. Every Friday five musicians, all playing stringed instruments of some kind, would arrive for a concert. Beth was certain that such perfect sounds must surely be derived from heaven. Certainly, she had never heard its equal. There was also the explosive music of the man Catherine called that heathen German, Beethoven; Haydn's intricate symphonies, some composed for London audiences; Mozart—all names Beth had never heard before but which were whispered in the proper "circles," Catherine said.

Soon Beth owed a great deal to Catherine Claremont, so much that she could never fully repay her. The woman had tenaciously molded her until she had become that which she had so wanted to be. A lady. More importantly, however, was the fact that Beth had really begun to have a deep affection for the woman.

Clad in a thin linen nightgown, her hair falling loose about her shoulders, Beth sat now with her arms folded about her knees and her legs drawn up to her chest. Slowly her eyes touched on the blue canopy over her bed. A dressing table covered in a cloth of the same shade of blue stood in one corner. There was even a lamp with a round globe by which she could read whenever the urge struck her. So many comforts that she had once dreamed about were now a reality.

Beth rose and padded across the room on bare feet to look in the dressing table mirror. Was she expecting to see another face looking back at her? Yes. But the eyes, the nose, the mouth were still the same. Her face had not changed as greatly as her newly acquired manners. It was still the same Beth staring back at her.

"I'm still me!" And she would remain so. She would never allow herself to become some haughty snob, uncaring of the suffering that went on around her.

It was a normal London morning. Men were shouting, horses neighing, dogs barking, cats fighting, pie men calling, donkeys braying, market carts stirring up dust as they rattled by. Jamie listened to the din of the women chattering as they walked down the street, their straw baskets bulging with fruits balanced on their head. Everywhere Londoners were going to and fro to earn, or some to steal, their daily bread then fight their way back home again.

Advertising was everywhere, even on the sides of vacant houses or scaffolding. As he walked along, Jamie read the hand-bills to see if there was anything posted about that night at the inn, thankful that his mum had taught him such a skill. Thankfully, there was no mention of the incident, at least along this road.

"Off to the lanes, we are," Annie said coming up behind him and giving him a poke in the ribs. "Off we go."

Petticoat Lane, Rosemary Lane, Holywell Street, and Monmouth Street were the centers of the old-clothes trade and the markets. Since middle London was the older part of the city everyone passing from one district to the other had, at some time or other, to go through the run down areas frequented by thieves.

Garbed in an old hat, pulled down low over his forehead, and a fake beard, Jamie walked beside Annie as they went in search of his "wardrobe."

"We'll get yer good enough clothes to rival any bloody duke. Ye'll be bloody beautiful, James. Beautiful," Annie proclaimed. She poked him in the ribs again. "So yer see, lovey, I'm not 'oldin' yer mistake at the inn against yer."

He grimaced at the reminder, somehow wishing he had been able to keep it a secret. Despite having been Annie's lover, he wasn't certain that he trusted her completely, especially as a business partner. She had a violent, destructive temper that had harmed many a man and woman who had not done things her way. Still, he had to admit that he had little other choice.

"I need just enough frock coats and trousers to start me on me waiy!" He didn't want to be greedy.

Annie patted her money pouch hidden beneath her petticoats to keep it safe. "Me boys and girls 'ave been lucky. I've enough to buy yer anything yer want, Jamie dear. And a little something for meself."

A low necked dress, something more stylish, an imitation of the ladies of quality she saw walking daintily along the streets was Annie's first acquisition. She owned several stylish dresses, which she alternated as the mood suited her. Today she wore pale green linen with puffed sleeves. Her choice of a hat was a bonnet with a soft crown and rigid brim.

As for Jamie, he was elated at the finery he found presented to him. It was quality merchandise. Indeed, why not. Most of it had been stolen from the baggage and homes of the rich so that it could bring a profit here. But who would know? As long as he made certain he didn't pick out any monogrammed article of clothing he would be just fine.

"Oh, look Jamie!" Annie held up a tobacco colored frock coat with a dark green cravat. "And this!" She had the enthusiasm of a girl as she displayed another find. A waistcoat of blue and black stripes.

Jamie found several of his own favorites—a dark blue frock coat, tan trousers with narrow legs and a front fly with all of the fastenings intact. He picked out three pairs of boots, brown, black and tan leather, and two pairs of leather shoes. As for hats, he picked two—a top hat and one of the new "bowlers." Two white shirts, five pairs of socks, long underdrawers, a black cravat and a pair of black trousers completed his wardrobe along with gloves, waking canes, fobs, a watch, and an umbrella. With their arms filled with packages, Annie and Jamie headed to Covent Garden.

Covent Garden hummed with voices. Wagons and carts had been arriving for some time, thus various sellers were busy transferring their contents to the different stations of traders called *costermongers* and setting up displays. Produce was assigned to one area, flowers and plants to another, hens and chicks to still another. There was a separation of different classes of articles. Carts and wagons of vegetables; fresh cabbages, onions, leeks, potatoes, clean-washed turnips, carrots, and cauliflowers were drawn up close together on three sides of the market.

"I'm 'ungry. Ow about you, eh, Jamie?" Annie pilfered a few of the more appetizing eats.

The west side of the square was covered with potted flowers and all sorts of plants in bloom. Cut flowers for bouquets, tiny buds for nosegays, and potted plants still enrooted, were artfully arranged. Little tables were set up with refreshments by vendors of tea and coffee. Jamie's first filch of the day was a hot brimming cup, artfully hid behind him until he could safely savor its contents behind a pillar of the piazza. Peering out, he scanned the gathering crowd. Nobs, most of them. All turning up their noses at the likes of he and Annie. Well, not for long.

The air was filled with the fragrance of flowers and he sniffed with a contented sigh. Sweet briar and roses gave out such a delicious aroma. Giving in to a romantic mood he bought a small bouquet and presented it to Annie.

"Roses for a rose," he said.

"Awwww, Jamie," she was visibly touched. Even a hard-as-nails businesswoman such as Annie was softened by the sight of a flower. It was something Jamie had learned from his mother and which he had vowed to remember

As usual the streets of London seethed with traffic—wagons, carriages, and coaches sending the pedestrians fleeing as they rumbled down the road. Streets in the poorer area were in such deplorable condition that ruts and holes were filled with sticks and straw and the streets were so narrow that only one vehicle could get by at a time. Was it any wonder the drivers swore such violent oaths?

Jamie and Annie were forced off the street time after time, narrowly escaping serious harm to their persons. "Blimey!" he breathed, stepping back into the shadows as one particular carriage passed by, not because of his close brush with injury, but because of the woman who looked out from the window. Auburn haired and smiling, she was dazzling. One of the prettiest women in London, or so he told himself. "Who?" He pointed after the retreating carriage.

A man standing behind him quickly answered. "Catherine Claremont, 'at's who."

Jamie's heart seemed to leap up into his throat. He was certain that its loud and rapid beating sounded like a drum to passers by. "Who?"

"Catherine Claremont," the man said again. "I used ter work for 'er did, as a gardner."

"You are sure?"

"As sure as I am of me name." The man hurried off.

So, that was Catherine Claremont. No plain-faced sinister, this one. A myriad of emotions flooded over Jamie. Strange, how their paths had crossed twice now, as if it was meant to be.

"Jamie, wot on earth is wrong?" Annie punched him in the shoulder, angry at his inattention to her.

"I'm sorry, Annie. I've got a lot of things on my mind." In truth he did.

Six

Snuggling against his pillow, Jamie gave himself up to the same dream that had floated through his sleep the last several nights. Music reverberated through the night and he was dancing, whirling round and round, holding in his arms, first one woman and then another—all elegant of course.

"Oh, James, you dance so divinely."

"And you are the most beautiful woman here," he was saying to the woman in the white lace gown. He shivered at the intensity of his voice. "That gown brings out the luster of your hair, the pink softness of your mouth. I'll never let another man claim you, Catherine. Never! You belong to me . . ."

She was close to him, her breasts brushing against his chest. He felt bold, he felt powerful, he felt impassioned as the music reached a crescendo and he spun her around and around. He dipped her over his arm with a husky laugh, drawing her closer. His lips caressed the soft curve of her shoulder where her skin lay bared. He wanted her. Oh, Lord, how he wanted her.

"Some say that you are a duke in disguise. Or perhaps even a foreign prince. Your speech is so perfect, your manners so flawless." She sighed. "Who are you, James? Who are you, really?"

"Perhaps it will be more intriguing if I let my identity remain a mystery."

"Mystery?"

His fingers tightened on her shoulder, his mouth hovered only inches from her own. Taking a deep breath, he awaited the kiss. A kiss that never came.

"Ahhhhh! 'Tis you!"

Several pairs of eyes accused him. "Me?"

"The rogue who killed the man in the inn-yard."

"No!"

"It is!" Their voices taunted him. "I know what you did. You took something that wasn't yours, then murdered him."

"No, I didn't." Suddenly every eye in the room turned his way, accusing him.

Jamie was rudely awakened as a soft hand caressed his face. "Bad dream, lovie?"

"No . . . no." He struggled to open his eyes. Dear God, they'd suddenly realized who he was! They would expose him, give him away. They would. "No!"

A strange, unfamiliar emotion pulsated through his veins. Remorse? Fear? He'd be sent to Newgate or worse. "No, I didn't . . ."

"Oh, but yer did," Annie was saying softly. "Yer instigated the best scheme in all the world, yer did. And I 'ave 'ired a teacher ter come ter yer this very daiy." She kissed him on the cheek. "Sir James."

"Sir James." Under the scrutiny of her stare he blushed. "Well now, maybe we won't go as far as that."

"And then, maiybe again we will." Annie laughed joyously, a thing she did often now. He had given her hope. "I believe in yer, Jamie. There isn't anything yer can not do."

Ah, but there was. As Jamie stared at the flickering candle he felt foolish and more vulnerable than he had felt in a long, long time.

"Say it correctly. Don't drop your consonants," the teacher scolded. "Don't make this any harder than it already is."

The candle's flame flickered and fluttered as Jamie diligently practiced the diction lessons. " 'Ow 'appy the little 'en . . ."

"No! No! No!"

*"H*ow *h*appy the little *h*en. Say it again!"

" 'Ow 'appy the little 'en . . ."

The stern, bespectacled instructor lightly spanked him on the hand. "Wrong! Again."

Jamie tried and tried, but to save his soul he couldn't seem to get it right. He tried to hide his shame with humor. He winked at Annie, saying "So glad the big ole rooster was when 'he . . ."

The levity did not work. The teacher, a woman in her late fifties was not taken in by Jamie's charm. She pushed and prodded him with no compassion or leniency. Soon Jamie pushed himself as well.

"*How happy* the little *h*en will be when she 'as . . . *has h*er chicks back in the blinkin' nest." He spoke the same sentence over and over, forcing himself to remember the "h" was not silent but spoken.

"Good!" Annie at least was delighted.

"Aye but I feel like a bloody fool, I do."

There were other rules as well, things like not leaving off his "g's" and "t's" at the end of a word.

"Not blinkin' but blinking." Or so the teacher said. "The letter "a" has many pronunciations, for example the short tone, "ah" as in the words "father" and "rather." There are also times when it takes on a long tone."

"Long?"

"Ay" as in "day" or "pray.""

"I praiy . . . er, pray this lesson is over soon," Jamie quipped. And indeed he did. Learning to talk like a gentleman seemed to be no easy matter.

"Pray if you will, I expect you to practice your "h's." I'll expect you to have them perfected the next time we meet." With a haughty glance at her surroundings, the instructor flounced out of the room. The room reverberated with a resounding bang as she slammed the door behind her.

"Oh, don't mind 'er. Today was splendid."

Annie was proud of him and determined that he would soon have his "h's" mastered.

How h . . . happy the little hen will be when she has h . . . her chicks back in the nest," Jamie said with a chuckle. The flame danced merrily with each correct sound. "How happy the little hen will be when she has her chicks back in the nest."

"The waiy we talk marks us, Jamie." The way she said it sounded as if Annie had never really realized that before.

"Aye, it does." Striding across the room he touched Annie's arm. "You can learn, too, Annie. If the old *h*en teaches me then she can teach *you*."

"No." Annie's expression was wistful. "You and me are different, Jamie my dear. Yer be meant for greater things than I. Somedaiy yer will leave me behind. I know it."

"I won't."

"Yer will." She said it so strongly that it sounded like an eerie premonition.

Part Two

A Game of Hearts
London-Winter, 1850

For when the One Great Scorer comes to write against your name,
He marks—not that you won or lost—but how you played the game.

—Grantland Rice, *Alumnus Football*

Seven

Sitting on a pink, satin cushioned window seat in her bedroom, Beth Longley watched the frost form slowly on the glass and sighed. Winter had set in. Cold. Bleak. Though there was usually very little snow in London, the frequent rain, days of fog, chilled air, and muddy streets made it extremely unpleasant. Beth found that in the elite areas the people had a better time of it, but she remembered that in middle London and the poorer areas of the city, the people would be enclosed together in cramped spaces like sheep. Summer with its clear sunny mornings seemed so far away.

"So much has happened . . ."

More and more she was being treated with all the deference of a relative instead of a paid companion. Her wardrobe had changed, her hairstyle, her way of walking, talking, and smiling. She had even been given lessons in how to sing, a pleasant addition to her other lessons, after Michaels, the butler, had heard her humming while at her dusting. He had drawn Catherine Claremont's attention to the pleasant sound. Now a cherubic-looking tenor prompted Beth to do scales and sing madrigals twice a week. Dubbing her a soprano, the instructor had invited Catherine to sit in on the lessons to add a breathy alto harmony as Douglass took the bass part and he the tenor line.

Clad in a thin linen nightgown, her auburn hair falling loose about her shoulders, Beth sat with her arms folded around her knees and her legs drawn up to her chest.

"I wanted to be a lady and now I have my chance," she breathed, turning from the window to stare into the dying embers of a hearth-fire.

Beth was enjoying the finer things of life. Even so, she had not forgotten Ruth or the others she had lived with. But although she had wanted to go back to them, Catherine had been most adamant in her arguments—the city was rife with thieves, murderers, and the like.

"Stay here and be safe," she had insisted. Catherine had, however, given generous gifts to Beth's friends. "You must put London's West end streets behind you."

Beth agreed, all the while vowing that once she had made her own fortune she would help them. As for now, Catherine had made her an offer of a home. Why then should she let pride goad her into refusing? Moreover, it seemed she was really needed, for Beth sensed a loneliness deep within this wealthy woman. Perhaps they were both lonely.

Her senses succumbed to the melancholy of the day. Encircling trees, skeletal now, rustled in the wind and cast eerie shadows on the ground, like outstretched arms. Nearby a rabbit bounded about, searching for food. The animal made a few aimless circlings, then settled itself by a bush, gnawing at bits of greenery left untouched by the cold. Just like Ruth and the others it was a survivor. Beth leaned forward as a dog suddenly gave chase, her eyes intently following the rabbit's path until it disappeared into the safety of a hole at the side of the carriage house.

"That's strange!" Beth leaned closer to the window. There was a tall young man loitering about Catherine's property, staring toward the house. "Who is he?" She wondered if he was building up the nerve to ask for employment, or if he had something more sinister in mind. Remembering Catherine's warning, she shuddered. Should she tell Michaels?

The decision was taken out of her hands. As if sensing the eyes that watched him from the street the tall figure darted into the shadows.

"Strange." She stared after him for a long, long while, then slowly her eyes touched on all the beautiful furnishings around her.

Beth sighed, wondering what her father would think if he could look down from Heaven and see all that she now had.

A knock interrupted her reverie.

"Beth!" It was Catherine Claremont's voice, "Are you in there, dear?"

"Just a moment."

Catherine Claremont had the look of a cat who had swallowed a canary as Beth opened the door. "I think its time you met some young men, or at least made yourself available to meet some."

"Young men?" Beth put her hand to her throat, shaking her head. "I . . . I don't want to. She conjured up recollections of the pinches and pats she had suffered during the last few years. "I'm . . . I'm not. . . ."

"Ah, but you are. Besides, I can't imagine your preferring to stay home instead of seeing one of Mozart's operas."

"Opera?" She was intrigued. "Which one?"

"I'm going to surprise you. That is, if you want to go. Do you?"

She answered without hesitation. "Oh, yes!" If that meant putting up with some ogling swain, well, so be it. The music would be worth it.

"Good."

There was a refreshing innocence about this child despite her unfortunate upbringing. The girl always delighted her. Beth was poised, intelligent, mannerly and so straightforward about what she thought that it was refreshing. Catherine Claremont had begun to look upon Beth as the daughter she'd wanted but never had. A young woman of fortitude and a kind heart.

"I'm glad."

Catherine Claremont studied Beth for a long moment. The young woman was a marvel, and she learned so quickly. And Catherine had more than one surprise in store. She had secretly conversed with one of her dearest friends, a woman with a very eligible son. He was to meet Beth at the opera, and if everything worked out, Beth soon would be a member of a very influential family.

Like the metamorphosis of a caterpillar, Jamie was slowly shedding his old ways and becoming a gentleman, thanks to the elder woman's tutelage, a woman he had dubbed "pruneface." He had grown a mustache, partly to celebrate this change and partly to hide his identity just in case he was seen during the day.

It had been a slow transformation that had threatened to snuff out his patience. Slowly, however, and surely his once nervously stumbling and stuttering tongue had ceased tripping over new words and pronunciations. With carefully placed teeth and tongue he now formed his consonants and vowels in a well-modulated tone.

"It's not so much what you say, my dear," the instructor had told him with a wry smile, "but *how* you say it. To move in the proper circles you must learn to speak correctly." Scathingly she eyed Annie up and down.

Jamie learned when to listen attentively and when to voice an opinion, how to nod his head politely in agreement or to shake it slowly, when he disagreed. It seemed the "swells" as he called them, abhorred argument of any kind. It was important for him to remember *never* to raise his voice. A show of temper was a sign of ill-breeding.

Even Jamie's laughter had been the object of a lesson. It was less guttural now and had a mellow ring to it.

To remind Jamie to stand up tall, shoulders thrust back, a board had been strapped to his back. Now, his walk was dignified, his posture stately, his poise commendable and unshakable in most instances.

"And now, you must learn how to dance properly. The waltz. It is a dance that you must master."

"Dance?" Jamie broke into a vigorous approximation of a sailor's jig. His tutor frowned.

"Suitable for a mariner's revel, perhaps. But not a ballroom."

Jamie ceased capering, and let the grim woman lead him to the center of the worn floor, not without a visible shudder down his spine.

"The waltz is a glorious creation. And quite romantic, I dare say."

"Romantic." Jamie scoffed.

"Let us begin."

Jamie followed her lead, feeling very proud of himself. He had almost mastered the fine art of being a gentleman. Now he had only to find his special woman to woo.

Eight

Covent Garden Opera House was bursting at the seams with those who wanted to see Mozart's opera. It was hardly surprising that Beth was excited by the prospect of being at the theatre with Catherine Claremont.

"Perhaps soon it will be a handsome young man at your elbow, not some doddering old woman," Catherine said laughing as she gave Beth a gentle prod.

Money was being taken at the gate by a money-taker. People were standing in line, pushing and shoving, waiting for the doors to open. As they crushed through the crowd, Beth was suddenly thrust against a man's chest. For just a moment he held her against him, imprisoning her in his strong arms as he gazed smilingly down at her upturned face.

For just a moment in time she was all too aware of the hardness of the man's body, searing her through the silk of her gown. "Excuse me. . . ." Beth stammered, pulling away. It had been but a brief embrace, yet long enough for her to realize how avidly the man had been staring at her.

"I do think that handsome dark-haired man has eyes for you," Catherine Claremont whispered in her ear. "Perhaps. . . ."

Beth blushed, quickly putting the man out of her mind. Little did she realize that he most definitely did not want to forget her. "Who is that?" Jamie asked, pointing, wanting to confirm the identity of the beautiful woman so briefly held in his arms.

"Catherine Claremont," a man answered, following the line of his finger.

"She . . . is rich?"

"Rich?" The man looked at him quizzically. "Of course. She is a very rich woman."

"Married?"

"Widowed," came the answer.

Jamie clucked his tongue. "By Jove, what a shame." He smiled, looking the auburn-haired woman up and down with admiration. "Well, perhaps she won't be alone much longer." As he walked down the aisle he was walking on clouds. If he played his cards right he would soon be a real gentleman in every sense of the word, with a beautiful woman on his arm.

The theatre smelled of tallow, glue and the fragrances of ladies' perfumes. Below Jamie could see those of lesser means meandering through the inexpensive middle gallery. They were not as elaborately dressed or as well-mannered. Indeed, when a song or character did not please them they often threw things to show their disapproval, or so he had heard it said.

Jamie knew that pickpockets often roamed about the audience, waiting to find the right prey. He clutched his once-pilfered money pouch tightly as he walked. He eyed the men he was rubbing elbows with. Their rings, heavy watches and fobs, the seals hanging singly or in pairs from a waistcoat pocket once would have made his fingers itch. Now he had more important things to think about, such as an introduction to the lovely young woman.

Catherine Claremont led Beth to a private box. Beth forgot all else in the excitement of the moment, staring in amazement at the gathering of society's elite, forgetting for the moment that she was every bit as fashionable. Dressed in bright blue taffeta, her bell-shaped skirt swirling around her as she took a seat, she was a vision of beauty and elegance, thanks to Catherine.

Catherine was pleasantly amused by her young companion's wide-eyed interest. It was as if she were seeing the theatre through her eyes. "Well, what do you think?" she asked.

The stage was lit by fixed strips of candles behind the proscenium arch. The candlelight gave off a special glow. "I think it's grand!"

"I hate to admit it, but most of the people gathered here do not share enthusiasm for seeing this opera. The object is to be seen and to see, I'm afraid, not to watch the performers." Again she smiled. "Indeed, I would say that they come to view each other's finery and to gossip."

"Indeed." Anxiously she looked about her, startled when a young man across the theater waved. It was a shocking display of bad manners, or so Catherine whispered in her ear. Still, it seemed that a man as handsome as that one could be forgiven, especially when he obviously was smitten.

There was an expectant hum as the audience settled in their seats. The curtains were still drawn but Beth was fascinated by the musicians plucking and tooting as they prepared for the overture.

The murmur of conversation died away as slowly the house lights were snuffed. Stillness settled over the scarlet and gold room. The orchestra struck up the first faint strains of the overture. The curtain was down but the music that suddenly filled the enormous room caused Beth to shiver. She felt as well as heard it, each vibration touching her soul.The music reached out to her, soothing her, relaxing her. Slowly she closed her eyes, caught up in a web of enchantment.

After the overture the curtain was slowly drawn up. Beth had never seen anything quite like it before. Bright costumes, dancing, singing. Even though she couldn't understand exactly what was going on she was enjoying herself. She'd seen mimes and acrobats before, because they performed often enough in the streets and marketplaces, but this was different. She was completely entranced. The stage was like a bright oasis, each hue intensified by the brilliant candlelight.

"I think the *Magic Flute* is one of my favorites."

"I like it, too." Beth had to confess, "Although I can not tell what they are saying."

"Nor can I. I know a smattering of foreign languages because of my travels. This opera is in German and not Italian, though I think I prefer the softer tongue. Even so, this is a delightful work of art. Mozart was a genius. I'm told that this one is written in the form of a singspiel, a German ballad opera with spoken dialogue instead of recitative."

"Oh?"

"The story concerns the Queen of the Night who gives a magic flute to the prince, Tamino. He offers to rescue her daughter Pamina from the palace of the high priest Sarastro. Tamino finds Pamina, and also discovers that Sarastro is not evil, but a magnanimous priest of Isis and Osiris. A love story, you see. Most operas are." Catherine nodded toward where the young man was sitting as if already expecting something to happen with him eventually. "The priest permits Tamino to undergo the ordeal of the search for truth, but he is not supposed to say a word."

"And does he find Pamina?"

"Of course. He is aided by Papageno, a birdman who plays a magic flute. But she is mystified by his silence and nearly kills herself because of unrequited love. But because it is a happy story, she does not do the deed, the lovers arrive at the temple of success and Sarastro blesses them. Both pairs of lovers live happily ever after."

"Both pairs?"

"Papageno finds a bird girl. Which goes to prove that there is someone for everyone on earth if they are only fortunate enough to find them."

Beth was glad of that. Certainly everyone in life deserved to find love.

"The Queen of the Night's aria I find particularly stirring. It takes a voice with a wide range and of course great talent. It is rumoured that Mozart was a Mason, and that this opera embodies Masonic ideals, but I wouldn't know for certain."

"Masons?" Beth took her to mean those who worked with brick and stone. She laughed. "How odd."

The evening moved on much too quickly for Jamie's liking. Acts One and Two were concluded and the last act had begun.

What did it matter? He hadn't seen one moment of the opera. He had been too intrigued with *her*. Indeed, he could have spent every minute of every day just looking at the lovely Catherine Claremont. One thing he knew for certain, she was the *one*. He wanted very much to court her. But how was he to begin?

"She has beautiful breasts," he thought to himself. Her bodice was laced in front with ribbons and his fingers trembled as he thought how much he would like to untie them. But what hope had he of ever touching her if he did not get up the courage to approach her? It was a problem that tortured him as he sat through the opera, but at last when the opera was over he somehow found the nerve. Remembering his instructions he made his way to Beth's side and gently took her hand.

"I have been watching you from afar," he whispered in her ear.

"Yes, I know." She laughed softly. "But pray tell why?"

"Because you are the most beautiful woman I have ever seen." Seeing her up close he knew what he said was true. Never had he seen such soft, unblemished skin or lips so perfectly shaped. Or eyes that shone like sapphires in the night. Fascinated, he took her hand, his lips lingering on her soft flesh as he kissed it.

Catherine was elated. It was obvious how taken her friend's son was with Beth. He had stared at her all night. It was going even better than she had planned.

Beth didn't know what she thought of this forward young man, still she had to admit that he was undeniably handsome. Remembering her manners she started to introduce herself. "I'm . . ."

Jamie smiled. "I know who you are." Her name had played upon his lips since the first time he had seen her.

"You do?" Beth cocked one brow. "Well, sir, I do not know you."

Thinking carefully before he said each word, lest he make a mistake in his speech, he introduced himself. "I'm James." He whispered in her ear. "But you can call me Jamie."

"James?" The real Catherine Claremont broke in.

Seeing her look, fearing that somehow his past might catch up with him, Jamie told a white lie. " 'Tis my middle name."

She brightened. "Oh!" Catherine studied him for a disconcerting moment. "You greatly resemble your father."

Jamie stiffened. "Ah, yes." He played along with the game, wondering who this woman with Catherine could be.

Catherine smiled. "You remind me so of him. I think it's the way your eyes crinkle just like his, when you smile."

Jamie nodded. "It is! It is."

Hoping to quickly initiate a romance, she whispered in Beth's ear, telling her to ask the handsome young man to the house for dinner. It was an invitation Jamie quickly accepted. He didn't have to be asked twice.

Again Catherine smiled. "Say hello to your mother for me!"

"Me mum?" he whispered, forgetting his proper speech in the emotional turmoil of the moment. "My mother?" he corrected. The reminder of the woman he had so dearly loved hurt his heart. As he watched the two women walk away he couldn't help wondering what his mother would think if she knew what he was planning.

The smells from supper lingered, mixing with smoke from the kitchen stove, stale wine and ale. All these odors assailed Jamie's nostrils as he pushed open the heavy door.

"How dismal!" After having been near the beautiful Catherine Claremont, the place where he lived seemed all the more depressing. What would Catherine think if she knew his circumstances? He wouldn't tell her, not until after they were married. Once she loved him she would understand.

"Ah, so there 'e is. Romeo!" Dressed in a flannel nightgown, her hair hanging free, Annie looked much younger than her thirty-five years as she swept forward. "Well, don't just stand there. Tell me wot 'appened."

Strangely enough, despite their plans, Jamie didn't want to

talk about it. It was something he somehow needed to keep private. "Everything is fine!"

"Fine?" Annie circled him. "Lord love a duck. Wot do yer mean by fine?"

"She . . . she invited me to dinner tomorrow night," he answered.

"She did!" Annie was elated. Throwing her arms around him she hugged him tightly. "Yer charmed 'er. But then I knew that yer would." She clung to him for awhile, then studied him when she stepped away. "Aw, Jamie. 'Ow could I be so insensitive. Yer don't seem very talkative. That's rare for yer. Which tells me something."

Fearing she had read his attraction to Catherine Claremont in his eyes, Jamie looked down at his polished leather shoes. "What?"

"Poor, lovey. She must be a fright!" She shuddered. "But perhaps once yer 'ave married 'er yer won't 'ave to bed her very often. And when yer do yer can remember all that money."

"Yes, the money . . ." Jamie answered. There had been something in Catherine's eyes. A look of vulnerability. Somehow it made him feel like the world's biggest heel.

"Ah, but let's celebrate!" Muttering beneath her breath about how rich they were going to be, Annie filled two glasses with wine and quickly set them down on a nearby table. "There!"

"A celebration!" he exclaimed half-heartedly.

"And drinks for all of our boon companions," Annie insisted, calling them into the kitchen.

Soon the room was filled with a low-buzzing chatter as Tate, Clara, Freddie, Paddy and Ebenezer joined them.

"So, she's a rich one." Clara winked her eye, envious of any woman Jamie's eye had been set upon, even if it was because of her money.

"Moderately so," Jamie answered, trying to play the circumstances down. In actuality he knew very little about the Claremont fortune. His thoughts had been elsewhere tonight.

"Moderately rich," Freddie said enviously. "Maiybe she needs some 'elp wi' her luggage." He grinned evilly.

"Leave her alone!" Jamie gave a stern warning. "I don't want you or any of the others to go anywhere near her. Do you hear?"

The thieves looked at him wide-eyed, unfamiliar with this side of Jamie. "All roight!"

Annie was quick to come to his defense. "Jamie doesn't want yer all ter spoil anything fer 'im. Were she to find out about anything it could ruin it for the rest of us."

"Aw!" Freddie grinned, his eyes gleaming with merriment as he plopped his girth into a chair. The impact sloshed Jamie's wine all over the table.

"Be careful!" Jamie said, shaking his head. Something was grating on his nerves.

A grunt was his only answer. Then, picking up a glass and filling it to the brim he held it aloft. "To the future. May all nights be as profitable as this one has been."

"Or at least will be," Annie echoed. Raising her glass, she sipped the wine, mimicking the genteel manners of a lady.

Suddenly it seemed very quiet, with an oppressive silence that unnerved Jamie, as if everyone had stopped talking all at once. But it was not silent for long. Soon everyone was talking at the same time.

Jamie's eyes were hooded but a muscle ticking in his cheek betrayed his annoyance. Suddenly he wanted to be far, far away from here. If only that could be. And yet he was trapped. Like it or not, these people were his kind and he would do well to remember that.

Later, alone with Annie, his thoughts remained troubled. He wanted to be anywhere but here. He wanted . . .

"Annie!" He pulled her roughly against him. Slowly lowering his mouth he kissed her. He ran his hands down each side of her soft body, a body that tonight held no delight for him. All he could think of was a pair of wide blue eyes.

"Oh, Jamie!" Annie was looking at him with expectation.

Slowly, he removed his hands from her body, any desire he might have had quickly waning. "I'm tired," he said.

"Tired! You?" Throwing back her head she laughed. "Ah Jamie, wot game is this?"

"It's no game!" He shook his head.

A younger, less experienced woman would have been hurt. Annie merely smiled. "Well then lovey, go ter sleep and rest yerself. I'll wake yer up a little later. Eh?"

"You can try," he answered flatly. What was wrong with him? He had never turned Annie down before. She was a passionate lover. And yet right now all he could think about was a woman with a face as gentle as a nun's.

Nine

Beth watched anxiously from her bedroom window trying to take her mind off her nervousness. Why had Catherine Claremont encouraged that overbold man? Why had she had Beth ask him here to dinner?

"Oh, why . . ." It was obvious just what Catherine Claremont intended—that the young man and Beth would meet and become attracted to each other. Well, Beth felt a bit of stubbornness tweak her pride. She would be pleasant, she would be polite, but she did not want him to be interested in her. Matters of the heart caused too much turmoil with a person's senses.

She stood a long time at the window, catching sight of a trim black carriage as it came rolling up the road, turning at the carriage house.

"He's here!" She wondered just what he would be like in a less formal situation. Though she tried to convince herself that she just didn't care, the very thought left her breathless with anticipation. After all, most girls dreamed of finding their handsome prince. Perhaps this young man would be hers.

Leaning against the window she tried to catch sight of him but the leaves on the trees obstructed her view. All she could see was a dark-clothed form alighting from the carriage.

Opening the door of her bedroom, Beth listened to the sounds below—the rattle of the carriage as it pulled into the drive, the footsteps, the knocking. Moving to her dresser mirror she carefully checked her appearance. She approved of the image that stared back at her. Her auburn hair was parted in the middle, curving down over her forehead and below her ears where it looped up in braids to meet the bun placed high on the back of her head. Beth decided she approved of this new coiffure.

Wearing a dress with a V-waisted bodice or parchment-colored silk, the long sleeves of which were caught up at the shoulders, she looked most fashionable. The bodice had a narrow edging that decorated the oval decolletage, giving a view of the unblemished skin of her throat. A matching velvet belt nipped in her waist. The skirt, which was shaped like a bell, swept the ground, rustling as she walked across the floor to the door. A pearl necklace, loaned to her by Catherine, completed the outfit. Reaching up, Beth assured herself that it was still safely around her neck then smiled ruefully as she slipped out of her room and descended the stairs.

Jamie brushed off his coat, mentally making an account of what he had to spend for the carriage tonight. Oh well, Annie had told him not to spare any expense in this hopeful enterprise. Still, he hoped that this matter of wooing would be quick. He wanted to win the woman, marry her, and bask in the joy of wedded bliss.

"At least for a short time before she finds out that I am a fraud," he said to himself, forcing himself to smile as the butler said, "Come this way."

Michaels led him to the drawing room where the white-haired woman was waiting. Jamie passed his coat to the butler, all the while eagerly scanning the room in hopes of viewing his lady-love. Alas, she wasn't there.

"She is still dressing," Catherine Claremont said. "I fear that for the moment you are stuck with me."

"To the contrary." He judged the woman with an all-knowing eye. She was beautiful. In her youth she must have been able to give just about any woman a run for her money, so to speak. "I must say you look lovely tonight in that peach-hued gown. Surely the most attractive woman in all of London."

Catherine blushed under the scrutiny of his gaze. "You, dear sir, are a flatterer. But since I want to believe you, I will."

"As well you should." Jamie looked toward the stairs, staring speechlessly as a most stunning woman glided down the steps. "Beautiful," he breathed. More so than he had remembered. Oh, how jealous Annie would be if she could see. As it was, he had failed to mention it, allowing Annie to believe that the woman was plain-faced.

Beth touched her tongue lightly to her lips to ease the dryness, unaware of the provocativeness of her action. "Good evening." Every nerve of her body was vibrantly aware of him—his strength, his good looks. The pleasant hint of musk and leather teased her nose.

"Good evening."

Her heart thundered so frantically she thought it would surely burst. "Good evening." His eyes caressed her with a heat that stirred her blood and set her heart racing. How many times had she dreamed of falling in love? More than she could count. And now, suddenly, it did not seem to be such an impossible thought.

Catherine Claremont's cook prepared a veritable feast for the occasion. There was roast duckling in orange sauce stuffed with almond dressing, a side of roast beef, plates of steaming vegetables seasoned with herbs, a small loaf of bread, and apples, plums, and pears. It was enough food to feed a small army, though the table was set just for *two*. It seemed Beth's benefactress wanted this to be a romantic evening.

Two empty glasses awaited the bottle of wine that Jamie had brought with him. Pushing quickly into the dining room, he soon had them filled. He grinned and handed Beth a glass. "Lord love a duck, but you are something," Jamie said, forgetting himself. He clinked his goblet against hers in a toast, looking all about him in wide-eyed wonder at the wealth so artfully displayed all around him. So, the man at the theater had been right. This Cath-

erine Claremont was definitely not *poor.* What a lucky toff he
was to have found such "pickings."

Beth cocked her head, startled for just a moment by his lan-
guage. And yet, the way he poured the wine, the way he held
himself so erect seemed to indicate that there was nothing amiss.

Beth let her eyes appraise him. The candlelight emphasized
the planes of his chiseled features, the mystifying depths of his
eyes. In his gray frock coat and peg-topped trousers he made a
dashing figure. "I hope you are hungry," she said.

"Famished." And indeed he was. He hadn't had a bite to eat
since mid-morning.

"So am I, Mister Morgan." Beth took three long gulps of her
wine, letting it warm her. It gave her courage.

"James . . ." he corrected. Crossing his arms and putting one
foot up on a large stone of the hearth, he freely gazed at her,
trying not to be too obvious as he took note of the teasing view
of her breasts. Oh, she was a fine sight, all right—from the toes
of her dainty shoes to the top of her well-coiffuered head. He
took note of every detail, including her long, slim neck and the
perfection of her features. She was every inch a lady, there could
be no question of that, he thought taking a seat across the table.

He's staring at me, Beth thought. That made her nervous, so
much so that she hardly tasted the delicacies that passed her lips.
What was he thinking? "Do . . . do you go to the opera often?"
she blurted out, feeling more comfortable when there was conversation going on.

"The opera." Jamie wrinkled his nose. In actuality he had
never set foot inside a theater before, unless it was to con someone out of his wallet. He crossed his fingers and lied. "All the
time. And you?"

Whenever I can," Beth replied. Once, seemingly so long ago,
she had gone with her father. Later, when ill fortune had struck,
such enjoyment had been denied to her unless she sold flowers
inside the theater. "It's like another world."

"Aye, that it is," Jamie concluded with a long, drawn-out sigh.
One could only hope that real life would have such improbable

and fortunate endings. Such as a man from the East End of London marrying a beautiful heiress. He could only keep his fingers crossed. He always had been said to be a lucky bloke. Was he? Staring into her eyes he could only hope so. More so, however, was his wish that this lovely young woman would never have to find out about his past.

"What would she think if she did find out?" Jamie didn't want to even think about it. Still, as the evening progressed he found himself wanting to be truthful, at least with her. A woman so forthright, so honest just didn't deserve to be deceived.

"I . . . I . . ." For just a moment Jamie actually started to tell her the truth, then just as quickly thought better of it. No, he didn't want to be thrown out into the street, at least not yet. With that thought in mind he reached to take her hand.

It was as if a cocoon of enchantment enclosed them, a magic as potent as any poet could have dreamed up. As if they moved in slow motion, they noted infinite details about each other. She noted the way his eyes twinkled when he talked, the way he gestured so expressively with his hands. He noticed the way her cheeks dimpled when she smiled, the inquisitive way she tilted her head.

"The food. It . . . it was delicious," he blurted, feeling strangely tongue-tied for the first time in his life.

She'd hardly eaten a bite. "Yes, it was." Looking at her goblet she longed for another glass of wine. Anything to give her courage. "And the company truly delightful. I can never find the words to tell you how much I've enjoyed the time we've spent. Together . . ."

"Aye, together." Jamie felt an overpowering longing to kiss her. Still, he didn't want to rush things. Dragging his fingers through his thick dark hair he frowned, wishing he had had more experience with her kind of woman.

Suddenly shoving his half empty plate away he stood up, deciding to tell her the truth. "I'm not . . ."

Beth's eyebrows drew up in a "V." "You're not what ?"

Jamie lost his courage. "I can't stay too long. You're just too

tempting. The truth is that all this time I've been struggling with
the fact that I desire you. Very much."

His forthrightness stunned her and she dropped her spoon.

"Being here alone with you like this brings out my carnal
nature, I fear. The wolf in me." He stood up and headed for the
door but paused to look back at her. "I came here with the thought
of collecting a kiss, but now I realize how difficult it would be
to stop once I started."

"Oh" Beth blushed all the way to the roots of her hair. Still,
she admired his honesty. And after all, she was drawn to him,
too. In the fathomless depths of his eyes she saw a stirring of
passion that drew her to him. Reaching out she gently touched
his arm.

Jamie shivered, whispering her name. "Oh, Catherine . . ."

"What?" With a gasp, Beth pulled her hand away, realizing
the truth. Dear God, somehow he must have assumed that she
was Catherine Claremont.

Jamie lay in bed, stating up at the ceiling as he listened to
Annie's not-so-quiet snores. What was he going to do? How was
he going to handle this matter of falling in love?

Slowly he sorted out his thoughts and emotions. He was totally
and unabashedly taken with the Claremont woman. Money or
no money he was smitten, which was a frightening thought con-
sidering how vulnerable that always made a man. And yet, why
should he worry? Catherine wasn't the type of woman who would
put a ring in his nose and parade him around London. She was
sweet, truthful, and compassionate.

Truthful.

The word stung him. And yet, he hadn't really lied about who
he was. Mainly because no one had really asked. No, she and
the older woman seemed to think he was someone else. A friend's
son. A real gentleman.

He would be crazy to tell the truth. He was so close to attaining
all his dreams. Could he risk that?

Turning over on his side, he sighed. No, he couldn't, for if he did, if he once bared his soul there would be no turning back. Things said couldn't be unsaid. If he lost Catherine he might never win her back.

"I can't." The very thought made his throat go dry.

She had become so special to him so soon. Or was it really that quickly? Hadn't he fantasized about holding her in his arms since the first time he had seen her? Yes, he had. She was the very embodiment of all his dreams, everything he had ever wanted.

In her sleep, Annie reached over and brushed her hand against his arm, a reminder of who he really was and the kind of life he had led. So different from Catherine's.

"I don't want to hurt her!" he thought in torment.

Indeed, he really didn't want to hurt either of these two women and yet he would, for there was no way now that he could keep them both. To do so was the worst betrayal of all.

"What am I to do?"

It seemed that he was damned before he had even begun. He didn't want to live a lie yet if he told the truth he would lose everything he desired. If he played false then he took the risk that Catherine would one day learn the truth of his past and hate him for it. And then there was the problem of Annie. What did he owe to her? To himself? To Catherine?

He had to tell Annie that he was falling in love, that this matter had gone far beyond just the matter of business. And yet if he did, he risked her jealousy and anger. There would be no assurance that his mistress wouldn't retaliate vengefully upon her rival.

"Oh, Catherine!" he moaned in a heavy sigh.

She was the woman he wanted to live with forever. He wanted to share his dreams with her, open up his heart to her, wake up in her arms, have children with her grow old with her beside him.

Putting his hands behind his head, Jamie reflected on his life, much of which had been wasted. He was a man who seldom believed in dreams. He held few illusions, for he knew all too well mankind's frailties. Now, however, he wanted to dream, wanted to open up his heart. He wanted a woman who would love him in return.

The first light of the sunrise painted the room with a rosy glow. Clad in a thin pale blue negligee, her hair loose about her shoulders, Beth sat huddled in a chair by the fire, her eyes fixed on the fading embers. How long she sat staring into the hearth she didn't know. Minutes? Hours?

"He thinks I come from his world." But she wasn't some wordly miss with a fortune of her own. She was a hired companion. An employee.

"I should tell him who I am!" In truth he would find out soon enough and then this illusion, this fantasy, would crumble.

Tensely, she glanced toward her turned-down bed but her mind had been too active, too troubled to permit sleep. Leaning her head back she imagined his strong arms holding her, caressing her, thoughts that sent tickling shivers up her spine.

"No!" She didn't want to feel this way. She wouldn't. The feelings that stirred inside her breast were certain to plunge her into dangerous waters. "You must never see him again," she counseled herself. "Tomorrow you must tell him so." And yet, how could she?

At last, seeking the safe haven of her bed, she pulled the covers up to her chin to bring warmth to her chilled body. She would tell him whenever he called that she could not see him. She would plead the weather, a headache, the chills.

"No!" It might not break his heart but it would break hers. Her mind, her heart, the very core of her being longed for him. Her body, lying warm and yearning for the touch of his lips, rebelled against her common sense. Desire was all too primitive and powerful a feeling.

Tossing and turning on her feather mattress, she could not keep her thoughts from him as she pictured every detail of the evening they had spent together. Swaddled in blankets where everything was soft and safe, Beth stared up at the ceiling of her bedroom. She couldn't sleep. How could she after what had happened tonight?

Beams of moonlight danced through the windows, casting figured shadows on the roof overhead. Two entwined silhouettes conjured up memories of the embraces she longed for. Wrapping her arms around her knees, she curled up in a ball, envisioning again the face of the man who haunted her even now.

She wanted to run away with him, to follow him to the ends of the earth if necessary, just to see him smile. She wanted to forget the past and begin anew. But it wasn't possible. She knew that with a frightening clarity. Sooner or later he had to find out that she was just plain Beth, a young woman with no relatives, no future, no hope. Would he then look so lovingly into her eyes? No!

Shivering, she slipped on a robe. Already the house was stirring. She could hear the watchman's bell in the distance and the Charley's loud voice calling out "all is well."

"What am I to do?" Her first instinct was to run away—to pack up her belongings and go where no one could ever find her. And yet she could not leave Catherine Claremont. Not after the woman had been so very kind to her. Besides, she had entrapped herself between two worlds, lifted herself from the streets and alleyways to the streets trod by satin-slippered feet.

Her predicament played on her mind as she hurriedly donned a russet-colored dress and hurried down the stairs to join her benefactress at the breakfast table. Just what *was* she going to do?

Ten

A lover's moon hovered like a coin in the sky. An omen? Jamie thought that it was. Though the streets surrounding Vauxhall Gardens were clogged with carriages, and the night was chilly, he was in high spirits. And why not? He was with a beautiful woman, there was a magic in the night and he had a feeling everything was going to work out just the way he intended it to. He'd made up his mind to kiss the lovely Catherine Claremont tonight.

Jamie smiled. At first he had paid court with a feigned passion but all too soon his passion had turned to genuine desire. The lovely auburn-haired lady fascinated him, enticed him. Not just because she was wealthy, oh no. It was much more than that. Money or not he had the feeling that she was the right woman for him. She was an enchanting mixture of spirit and shyness, sweetness and spice. She was a woman with whom he could share his life, his soul, his heart.

Vauxhall was a perfect place to begin a seduction. The grounds were spacious, and lovers could usually discover a quiet place beneath the tall trees in one of the walks away from the bright lantern lights and the noise of the orchestra. For those who were hungry or thirsty there was generally a vacant booth where they could enjoy a bottle of wine, a dish of tea, or a glass of Vauxhall punch. On special occasions there were fancy dress balls with dancing all through the night, something to keep in mind for the future. Best of all, it was not expensive. The price of admission was only a shilling, and thus it attracted myriad social classes.

The contagious high spirits of brightly dressed Londoners

bound for the pleasure garden, passing by in the open two-wheeled curricles and closed carriages, increased his feeling of euphoria. Even the air had a heady intoxicating aroma. Edging closer to Beth's side of the carriage, he took her hand.

"Have I told you that you look radiant tonight?"

Beth laughed "Several times."

"Then I'll tell you several more. You are lovely."

She wore a white woolen dress decorated with red and black embroidery, and a matching bonnet and cloak.

Beth bit her lip. She had come so very close to telling him she had a headache, but something had compelled her to come tonight. Was it so she could tell him the truth? That she was not Catherine Claremont at all but her impoverished companion? Someone who hardly had two shillings to rub together? Beth sighed.

"Vauxhall Gardens is as famous as the Garden of Eden," Jamie said, grinning at what he implied. More than a few lovers would be hidden in the shadows here tonight. He hoped that he and Catherine would be among them.

The gardens were usually crowded and tonight was no exception. Leaving the hired carriage driver to search for a place to park the carriage, Jamie guided Beth through the pleasure-loving throng of Londoners. Dense masses were congregated around a small building that reminded Beth of an open temple.

"This stands in lieu of a music room," Jamie said. As they strolled closer they could hear the trilled voice of a soprano as she entertained the lookers-on with an aria. Applause greeted her as she ended the song.

Hand in band they strolled along the broad gravel walks. Dressed in their finery, young men and women as well as those comfortably along in years, were laughing, chattering, and embracing. "All of London seems to be here tonight." Jamie was anxious to be rid of them and be alone with her. Ah, well, he must not rush the moment.

"James . . . what . . . what if I told you that I wasn't . . ."

He wasn't listening. A quartet of strolling musicians was walking by and he hailed them. "Come play a tune. The one about the maiden with hair the color of my lady's."

A brightly-clothed musician stepped forward eyeing Beth up and down. Strumming his guitar, he broke into a song about a tinker's daughter, ending with the verse:

> "On the green, green grass she laid her head,
> I gave her my heart and my soul.
> We made sweet love on the earth's fine bed,
> And now I will ne'er live alone."

With a strum, the musician ended his song, sweeping his feathered hat from his head as he bowed. Jamie rewarded him with a fistful of coins, feeling immensely generous.

The crowd promenaded the gardens in all directions. In the background was a well-shadowed avenue of trees where loving couples could walk and where the night air was tinged with the hue of romance. Even the bubbling of a fountain could be heard in the distance.

Following the sound of the fountain they reached the bank of a pond with a gigantic statue of Neptune and eight white sea horses. To the left of the god opened another avenue which fed straightway to "Fate," to "the hermit," and the temple of *Pythia,* where a woman in the guise of a gypsy reclined on a soft bed of hay under a straw-roofed shed. "A palm reader," Jamie said. "Would you like to have her read your future?"

The woman held out her hands, beckoning. "Readings. For the low price of only sixpence. You, my fine sir?" The gypsy was a comely woman with dark olive skin and black hair who eyed Jamie with hope.

"No!" Beth was afraid to know, fearful also that the woman might be able to see into her past.

"You don't want to know what awaits you?" Jamie shrugged his shoulders. Well, perhaps that was best, lest the woman sense the truth of his identity. "Come, let's move on."

The dwelling of the sage hermit was their next pause but no

one was permitted to enter. They stood on the threshold, from whence they could admire the scenery—mountains, valleys, precipices, all worked in canvas and pasteboard. The old man, with a white beard, long robe, and wooden staff looked as if he had walked straight from the pages of the Bible.

"Step forward and I will guide you to your destiny. Will you be wealthy or doomed to poverty? Happy or meet a tragic ending? Will there be a great love in your life or will you spend this life and eternity alone?" He pointed at Beth and she cautiously stepped past him, but Jamie moved forward.

"Let's see just what he says."

The white-haired man asked Jamie a few questions, disappeared, and then in a few minutes handed Jamie a carefully copied written prophecy of what was to come.

"It says things are not always as they seem to be. An astute philosophy." Jamie laughed. "It says that I will travel by boat. Mmmm. He also prophesizes that there is a beautiful woman in my future. One who will join with me to walk the avenues of my life. All in verses, written most colorfully."

Beth took the paper from his hand. "No one can really see into the future. It is folly to think one can." She'd gone to a fortune teller with her father once and he had promised a long life and prosperity to them both. A week later her father was dead.

Amorous couples sought secluded corners. Taking her hand, Jamie pulled her down upon a stone bench in front of a splashing fountain. "Don't look so sad. Please . . ." Jamie's voice was soft.

The next thing Beth knew she was in his arms. Her stomach churned in delicious anticipation of the pleasure awaiting. Catch happiness before it flew away. He could be her happiness, if only . . . Reach out for it. Forget about the past and begin anew. She could with him.

Something was happening over which she had no control. A feeling that pulsed in her heart whenever he was near. It was as if they were somehow bound by an invisible thread that was drawing her to him. Was there such a thing as fate?

Wrapped in each other's arms, they watched the water cascading from the fountain, mingling with the flecks of light created by the stars. He held her so tightly, so fiercely, that she could not break free. Beth realized that she did not want to as she buried her face in the hollow of his neck.

She started to speak, but before she had time, his mouth was upon hers, his firm lips parting her softer ones. The kiss was incredibly gentle at first, a touching of lips, but then his mouth fused with hers in a searing caress that left her trembling from head to toe at the delirious sensations sweeping through her body Beth's experience with men before now had been wet kisses and groping hands in the dark. Nothing had prepared her for the jolt of sweet fire that swept through her upon Jamie's kiss. Engulfed in a whirlpool of sensations, she somehow found herself reaching up to draw him closer, wanting to savor this tender assault. Shyly at first, then with increasing boldness, her tongue moved to meet the heated exploration of his.

She couldn't think, couldn't breathe. Her ears filled with a violent rushing sound. She was melting under the touch of his lips as her heart raced, then seemed to stop beating entirely. Dear God, she had never realized that kissing him would be anything like this. Under the intoxicating movement of his mouth, she forgot everything and concentrated on the moment she had dreamed about.

Jamie sensed her response and continued kissing her. His lips parted hers, searching out the honey of her mouth. She was soft, her fragrance of violets engulfing his senses. It seemed that his skin flamed where their skin touched. The passion of their kiss, the fierce hunger he felt shook him. Though he was not a lady's man in the full sense of the term, he had been with enough women to know that there was something very special about this one.

Taking his lips from hers, he gazed longingly into her eyes. "Catherine . . ."

The warmth deep inside her that had flowered instinctively at the sound of his voice now cooled. He had called her Catherine. How could she let him believe that she was a woman of his social class without losing all her self respect?

"I have a confession," Jamie was saying.

"I do, too . . . ," she said softly.

"I brought you here tonight in hopes that you would grant me a kiss." He untied the lacing of her bonnet and pulled it off. Slowly, luxuriously, his hand traced the curve of her cheek.

"And as you see, I have . . ."

Her hair was held atop her head by three pearl combs, but he pulled them loose. Entwining his long fingers in the thick strands of her hair, he sent her auburn tresses tumbling down her back.

"Lovely hair. So thick." For just a moment he gave himself up to the hungry desire that swept through his body, then stiffened as he regained his self-control. "You are lovely. I thought that from the first moment I saw you." His mouth swept across her cheek to the strands of her hair. Suddenly, fireworks burst across the sky causing Beth to jump. "I'm sorry, I should have warned you."

She clung to him, remembering the feel of his lips touching hers. "It's . . . it's all right." It was as if the heat of their embrace had sparked the explosion, a most dazzling, brilliant exhibition.

The gardens were bathed in a bluish light and the many thousand lanterns looked pale and very dreamlike. Fountains sprayed, reflecting the glittering light of the fireworks above. It was as if they were the only two people in the world for a moment, enjoying this shattering of the night, but dimly she became aware that there were other pairs of lovers kissing and looking up at the sky. She heard a girl laugh in the distance.

Jamie could not take his eyes from her. He watched with hungry intent the way her smile played upon her lips, the way her blue eyes widened with each spark that lit the night. He was absolutely mesmerized by her.

The fireworks lasted a long while then ended with a final flurry of light that trailed sparks of red, blue, yellow, and green across the sky. Jamie thought how his reaction to her nearness was nearly as powerful. The moment his lips touched hers, his body exploded with a surge of desire. Even so, there was so much more. He felt a yearning to give, to share, and yes, to possess.

Her mouth was achingly soft against his and for one instant he had nearly lost his head completely. The question was, what to do about it?

He prided himself on being a sensible man and yet one kiss had unleashed feelings he had never thought he would feel, an all consuming tenderness that tempered his now burning passion. She was not some bawd to be tumbled on the grass. Regretfully, he pulled away surprised by the thoughts that pummeled his brain. It was a longing that intensified as the night progressed. Being with her made him happy. He wanted her. Not for an hour, a night, but for forever.

Later that night when they had danced, kissed, and strolled the garden until their feet ached, she nestled in his arms as the carriage jostled and jiggled. Beth's eyes were closed as she leaned her cheek against the muscles of his chest, and he watched her sleep. This lovely, enchanting young woman who was touched by both innocence and passion, was the living, breathing answer to his prayers. How could he have ever thought anything was important compared to the exhilaration he felt just holding her?

Yes, he wanted her, wanted to marry her. Not for her money, but because of love. Something Jamie had never believed in before. His seduction of Catherine was proceeding as planned, but he dared not tell Annie that he had fallen in love.

Annie picked through the day's swag, while Jamie dosed fitfully at her side, dreaming of Catherine's sweet kiss. She plucked a piece of engraved paper from the pile in her lap, examined it carefully, and shook him awake.

"Jamie. Wot's this then?"

Jamie rubbed his eyes open. "An invitation."

"Ter wot?"

Jamie read the flowing script. "To a ball."

"Ohhhhhh."

They exchanged a long look.

"This invitation is like a ticket to the opera. It gets a bloke like me and whoever I'm with through the door." There was only one woman he would take.

The crystal chandeliers flickered like prisms, giving off a rainbow of glittering hues from red to blue, yellow to green, and various shades in between. The ballroom was a dazzling array of splendor. The flames of a hundred or more candles shone down on the polished white marble, and Jamie realized that he, like the other guests, was reflected in the smooth surface of the floor.

"Fancy that." He smiled at his image, and jauntily adjusted his cravat.

Looking about her, Beth's eyes touched on the elegance of the room as well. It was like something out of a picture book. Red brocade couches had been strategically pushed against the walls to enlarge the dance floor and give those who didn't want to waltz a place to rest. Red velvet draperies fluttered in the breeze of the open window, revealing terraces where fountains, some in the shape of huge fishes, spewed forth a stream of water despite the cold.

"What if the water freezes?" she asked.

Jamie grinned. "Then instead of waltzing we can go ice skating." He gave her a gentle nudge. Everything was perfect. Catherine was visibly impressed. The night was cold but clear. He felt smugly proud of himself for having such a fine idea.

And Catherine? She was beautiful! That was the most wonderful thing of all. She was a living dream. Her auburn hair was swept up into an artfully arranged composition of curls, held in place by a double strand of pearls. Her dress was of filmy white satin, hemmed with a collage of brightly colored threads. The curving neckline revealed the twin mounds of her full breasts enticingly. Unlike the other ladies in the room who flaunted their jewels, she wore only the pearls in her hair and pearl ear drops.

She was a charming combination of virginity and sensuality. She was the most beautiful woman Jamie had ever seen or probably ever would, he thought, eyeing her with possessiveness.

Every man there was certain to covet her. Every man including himself.

Everything did not go perfectly, however. For just a moment Jamie feared his masquerade might be exposed as he and Beth suffered through a maze of faces and handshakes. Who were these people? What if someone realized he didn't belong here? What if he made a mistake in etiquette? There were so many strangers anxious to judge everyone in the room by how they appeared and what they said.

Once these same people would have turned up their noses at him. Now they were greeting him warmly, though prying into the where's and when's and how's of his life.

Beth felt tense and ill-at-ease. She was out of place here. Could Jamie sense that? Did he see? Oh, but she wanted to make him proud of her, wanted him to fall in love with her just as she was falling in love with him.

"Shall we indulge in a dance or two?" Jamie asked, thankful that he had learned how.

"Yes."

She wanted to dance, laugh, and be gay. She wanted to put from her mind all thought of anything else.

In the great hall the dancing had begun, music Beth recognized as a waltz. Hopefully, Catherine Claremont had not been flattering her falsely. She wanted to be graceful.

"Come."

Jamie caught her in his arms and was whirling her onto the floor. Just as in her dreams she twirled faster and faster as faces sped by and colors blended into one another.

"Oh, Jamie . . ." She was breathless and laughing.

When the waltz ended Beth found herself held within the warmth of another pair of masculine arms. Then another and another claimed her, each vying for her attention.

Jamie watched her solemnly. Even in a room full of people she caught his eye over and over again. "Beautiful!"

Once more he led her onto the floor. "Your coming here with me tonight gave me hope that I have a chance of winning your

heart." As if to tempt her, he lightly kissed her throat "Do I?"
His eyes were compelling, robbing her of her will, her reason.

For a long moment they seemed to be dancing in slow motion,
just looking at each other as he held her hand. One could have
heard the world spin, it was so silent. As if all of the other people
in the room had disappeared and she was alone in the room with
him. At first he simply held her, then his strength moved her
across the floor.

He was a wonderful dancer, graceful despite his strength. Her
feet barely touched the floor as they waltzed, as if she was dancing on air. She felt the strength of his chest push against her
breasts, the muscles of his thighs burning through her gown, felt
the heat of his body enveloping her. The contact was searing,
evoking memories of the embrace they had shared at Vauxhall.
Being so close to him, with his arm around her waist, his mouth
brushing her cheek, sent her senses spinning with a mingled
feeling of pleasure and alarm. She was lost whenever he was
near. All her resolve gone as quickly as leaves in the wind.

Beth felt dizzy, so much so that she clutched frantically at his
shoulder for balance. Slowly, vibrantly she was bound by the
music's spell, a fragile silken thread that was woven about them.
For just a moment she allowed herself to forget who he was, and
what could happen if she allowed herself to love him. She gave
herself up to the moment. The look of passion in his eyes made
her believe herself to be all the things she'd longed to be. Beautiful. Proper. Alluring. Desired. The kind of woman a man like
Jamie Morgan could love.

His chin touched the top of her head. She was so fragile, he
thought. Yet she had an inner sense of strength about her. Certainly she brought out a sense of protectiveness in him. He
wanted to sweep her up in his arms, carry her off, and never let
her go.

"Catherine . . ." There were so many questions he wanted to
ask but suddenly felt tongue tied.

She winced as he whispered her name. Once again she felt

trapped. She wanted to tell him and yet . . . She wondered what he would think if he found out she was little more than the maid.

He heard the fabric of her gown rustle against her skin and felt a familiar flash of desire surge through him. Just being near her fired his passions. No other woman caused such a potent reaction.

"Catherine . . ." he said again. His face was shadowed but she could feel the heat of his gaze. His head bent, tempting her as his lips brushed against her own as if to remind her of what had passed between them.

My life, my love, she thought. For the moment all she knew was the touch of his lips, the current of expectation that swept through her. She could feel her heart beating so loudly she was certain he could hear it. She couldn't think, couldn't breathe.

Tell him you love him, an inner voice whispered. Take a chance.

Their gazes locked and she couldn't look away. An irresistible tide, the warmth of her feelings for him, drew her. How could she lie to him? "Jamie, I'm not . . ."

He silenced her with a kiss, then pulling away, he tugged at her hand. "What if we left this place? What if we went somewhere where people weren't staring and we could be alone?"

Her wide blue eyes questioned. "Where?"

"Do you feel daring?"

The dark, silent night was broken only by soft moonlight that touched the waters of the Thames as the barge slowly drifted downriver. Jamie leaned back against the fancy cushions taking Beth with him, snuggling close against her as they huddled beneath the blanket to guard themselves from the chill.

"A ride upon the Thames in the dead of winter. A brave act!" He whispered in her ear. "You're a woman after my own heart." As he spoke his arm tightened to pull her even closer, marveling at how right it felt to hold her in his arms.

"Am I?" she answered, fitting her head in the curve of his arm.

Seeing that the two young lovers needed their privacy, the bargemaster discreetly turned his head away, making no conversation on the short journey. Even the oarsmen allowed the couple privacy, concentrating all their attention of the push and pull of their oars.

The night mist lent an air of enchantment as London stretched out in a sparkling panorama of lights. Lanterns glowed in a kaleidoscope of soft flickering flames. The babbling waters echoed with song as sweet music drifted in the night breeze. It seemed a perfect night for love and Beth was caught up in its spell.

The cushion was soft beneath them. For a long moment Jamie stared down at her. She was so lovely, he thought, his eyes moving tenderly over her thick dark lashes, the finely wrought shape of her nose, the curve of her mouth. "You look like a vision conjured up by my dreams," Jamie whispered in her ear. "An auburn-haired angel. Are you real?"

"Very real and very happy at the moment." Beth waited breathlessly as he lowered his face toward hers. His mouth captured hers in a kiss that spoke of his longing. She gave herself up to him, her lips opening ardently under his to taste the sweetness of his kiss. Her arms crept around his neck, her fingers tangling in his thick dark hair. She felt lightheaded, happy. Everything was so perfect, so beautiful with her sea captain beside her. Love seemed to beckon, promising a whole new world.

Jamie was swept up in the moment, too. She was beside him and it was a mesmerizing experience. God, how he wanted to make love to her. His gaze slid slowly over her slim body, lingering on the rise and fall of her breasts. With a groan he reached for the soft swell of her breast, caressing it with gentle exploring fingers.

"I've wanted to touch you like this for so long. Since first I saw you," he said softly.

Beth shivered with pleasure. "And I have wanted you to touch me."

They lay together, quietly, contented just to be together for a long luxurious moment. His fingers reached inside her bodice to feel her warmth, stroking and teasing the peaks of her breasts until she moaned low and whispered his name. She yielded to his hands, those hands that searched the curves of her body.

Jamie was on fire for her. He wanted her to be naked against him, wanted to feel the warmth of her skin. He kissed her again, fiercely this time, allowing all the hungry desire that was clamoring for release to sweep through his body. He clung to her, wanting more than a kiss—so much more. Compulsively, tantalizingly, he slid his mouth down her throat, wanting her to desire him as much as he yearned to possess her.

"Were we only alone . . ." he breathed. And yet where could he take her? He had no house, not even a room of his own. And surely he could not take her to Annie's. At the same time, he could hardly be so forward as to suggest that he make love to her in her own bed, at least not yet.

Eleven

"I don't want to do it. Annie. She isn't a purse to be snatched up. She has feelings."

"Wot?" The voice was shrill.

"I said that I don't want to continue with this wretched scheme. Count me out!" He wanted to court Catherine Claremont honestly to share his life with her and not involve her in any way with Annie.

"Let me know how much I owe you. Somehow I'll find a way to pay." He looked her right in the eye. "I want out!" Catherine had given him hope for the future. He didn't want to jeopardize his chance for happiness.

Putting her hands on her hips, she snarled at him. "Just loike that!" She mimicked him. "Out!"

"Yes, out."

Her voice was scornful. "So, Jamie me boy, yer are starting ter believe all this foolishness. Yer are beginning ter think that yer are a toff." She stood on tiptoes and met him nose to nose "Well yer aren't, Mister High and Mighty. Yer are a thief just like the rest of us 'ere. A thief which owes me just about more than 'e can pay off in a 'undred years, or so I would saiy." She quickly ticked off his list of debts. "The carriage, the clothes, the "diction" lessons. Not ter mention the amount I 'ad ter give to get the bobbies off yer tail."

Jamie spoke slowly, trying to maintain his calm. "I know, Annie. I know."

Oh, he knew all right just what she was about. Far from being the benefactress she pretended, Annie had instigated a one-sided code specifying that while the whole group shared their takings with her, she didn't play by the same rules. Jamie knew well that she was stashing all her profits away.

"Maybe if I can find a job I can pay you back. Maybe . . ."

The room was shattered by her cruel laughter. "A Job. A Job the bloke saiys. Her eyes sparkled dangerously. "The only job ye will get is at Newgaite, my fine friend. One testing ropes." Putting her hands to her throat she mimicked a man being hanged.

Newgate! Annie knew just how to goad a man whose past had been less than honorable. Since childhood Jamie had gazed on the exterior of that prison, dreading what lay behind its rough, heavy walls and massive doors.

"So, do you want to put fetters on me, hurl me into debtors prison, Annie?" Jamie asked, curling his lip. "Or will it suffice just to keep me tied to you by blackmail?"

There was no answer, she just smiled, much like a cat toying with a mouse.

The situation was steadily becoming more uncomfortable. Jamie felt trapped. What had he gotten himself in to? He suddenly longed to be free of this entanglement, free of this place. But how?

"I warn you, Jamie me boy. I own ye. I *do*. Just like I own all the others." Patting him on the cheek she smiled. "So get used ter it, lovey."

Get used to it? Jamie knew he never could. Not now! Not after the blessed sense of love and peace he had felt the last few nights. Catherine had given him a glimpse of what he had been missing in his life. How then could he settle for this?

Suddenly the air inside the room seemed stifling. Jamie had to get some air. Thrusting his hands in his pockets he pushed through the door, shuffled down the stairs, and made his way outside. Oh, how could he have been so blind? How could he have actually thought he was living?

Jamie walked outside to get some air. There had to be something he could do, someway he could make an "honest bloke" out of himself. He was clever, he was ambitious, he was strong. Moreover, he wasn't a bad looking fellow, if he did say so himself. Surely there had to be some honest, enterprising venture he could undertake.

Let's see, he could be an actor, a hackney driver, a bobby . . . Suddenly, something caused him to stop.

Two men lurked near the doorway of a nearby building immersed in conversation. From their fine garments he could tell at once that they were not from around here. Who were they? One man in particular drew his eye. He was walking briskly in front of the door, pacing back and forth like a fat cat ready to pounce.

Jamie's heart leapt as he realized he'd seen this man before. It was the magistrate, the man whose money pouch he had so blatantly stolen. It seemed an eternity ago.

Jamie's blood ran cold. He had to do something and be quick about it before he was recognized and caught in the net. With that thought in mind he quickly darted from shadow to shadow, avoiding the circles of sunlight that threatened to give his presence away.

Suddenly he heard the dreaded words. "It's the thief. After him!"

Jamie bolted for an open window. Banging into tables, bumping into drunken patrons, he stumbled only once as he chanced to look back. Pushing through a back door he chose his avenue of escape, running for his life.

Up one street, down another, ducking behind barrels, slipping through open windows, he was fortunate that familiarity with his territory gave him the advantage. With a gasp he flattened himself against the cold stone of a building, listening cautiously. The din of heels and voices passed him by, yet he remained in his hiding place for quite a long while. When he finally emerged he realized that the laugh was on him.

"It wasn't me they were after!" Instead it was another poor soul who was being dragged along behind the magistrate's wagon as the horses moved along. Jamie knew well where they were headed and he shuddered. Newgate! Annie's pantomime of a hanging came quickly to mind.

"But it wasn't me." At least this time. Pushing his fears aside, Jamie contemplated his blessings. He was free for the moment and that at least was the important thing, at least for now.

The sun painted the room with a warm, radiating glow. She was as still as stone but she could feel the whole world quaking around her. Touching her fingers to her mouth, she remembered Jamie's kiss and sighed. A sweet ache coiled in her stomach. His warm caress of mouth and tongue had ignited a host of sensations. Desire. Something she had never really felt until she'd met him.

"So, dreams really can come true," she breathed. He'd held her so tenderly, as if she were infinitely precious to him. But was that just because he thought her to be someone whom she was not? What if he learned the truth? What if he found out that she wasn't a lady at all but just plain old Beth?

It didn't matter. She had to tell him of her lowly status. Better that than to have him continue to think that she was someone else. And yet, how could she not want to continue in this dream for just a little while longer.

"I think I'm in love with him." Was it possible to lose one's heart that quickly? It was. She wanted to run away with him, to follow him to the ends of the earth if necessary, just to see him smile. She wanted to forget the past and begin anew. Was it possible?

"You can't keep playing this masquerade. He has to find out, sooner or later. If you don't tell him then someone else will." Would he then look so lovingly into her eyes? No! He'd feel cheated. All her dreams would tumble to the earth.

How was she going to get up the courage to tell him? Perhaps Catherine would know. Beth hurried down the stairs.

Catherine Claremont was just finishing her porridge when Beth made her entrance into the room. "Good morning."

Beth slid into her place across from the woman. "Good morning."

Catherine picked at her breakfast with a spoon. "I would assume by your tardiness that you had a pleasant time."

"The gardens were beautiful even in the winter." Nodding to Catherine, Beth turned over her cup.

"And? Catherine had the countenance of a smiling cupid.

Beth spoke her words aloud. "Catherine . . . what . . . what if you met someone and through some terrible, strange, funny mistake they thought you were someone else? What would you do?"

Catherine regarded her thoughtfully for a moment, her gray eyes sharpening their gaze. "By the expression in your eyes I get the strange feeling that is just what has happened to you."

Beth heaved a sigh. "Yes."

"And you have decided that the truth won't do?"

Silently, Beth took several small bites of her muffin, averting her eyes. "It might have, had I not been so cowardly. I should have spoken right up but I didn't. "Now my problem is two-fold." A frown etched two verticle lines between Beth's well-shaped eyebrows.

"Mmmmm . . ." Catherine touched her mouth with the corners of her napkin. "Your young man."

Beth nodded

"And just whom, may I ask does he think that you are?"

Beth forced herself to take another bite of the muffin, washing it down with a gulp of tea. She had lost her appetite. "He thinks I'm *you*."

"Me?" Though she seldom giggled, that was exactly what Catherine Claremont did. "Oh, no my dear. He doesn't. He couldn't!"

"It is *not* funny!"

"No, of course not." Catherine quickly sobered. "You must tell him the truth."

"I know. It's just . . . just that I'm nobody."

"Nobody?" Catherine was incensed. "That's not true. You are a lovely, intelligent, charming young woman, one whom it pleases me to call friend."

"He's a gentleman."

"And a man. A man smitten by a lovely woman. A woman whom he would cherish by any name." She didn't want to think her matchmaking had gone amiss.

"Are you sure?" Beth tapped her finger with the spoon. "What if?"

"Then certainly he was not for you, was he?"

Beth shook her head. "No." In the end she was resolved to put things to right. Tonight.

Twelve

It was a dull, murky night shrouded by a light fog. Even so, the streets of London were swarming with hackney coaches, carriages, and silk-lined, leather sedan chairs, transporting splendidly dressed men and women to various destinations—theaters, taverns, cozily lighted inns, or perhaps to more intimate rendezvous.

The *nobs,* Jamie thought. As different from him as night was from day. They at least did not have to hide in the shadows. But *I* must. The brief interlude today had brutally reminded him of that.

"Catherine . . ."

The love that had briefly blossomed between them was doomed. How could he even think otherwise? Love could never be built on dishonesty.

"The moment she finds out what you really are, Jamie old boy, she will scorn you." Leaning against a large rain barrel, he knew he could never stand that. What was he to do, then? Just disappear from her life? No. That was the coward's way out. He had to somehow gather up his courage and tell her the truth. Well, at least part of it.

A bell from a tower somewhere in the distance tolled nine times. Even so, there were still a few vendors out and about. The baked-potato man, the kidney-pie man, the cheesemonger, all hoped to arouse appetites with their sing-song chanting.

"Baked potatoes. Hot baked potatoes."

"Kidney pie, fresh from the oven."

"Cheese . . . old enough to please . . ."

Several boys crouched in little knots in the projecting doorway, holding out their hands in supplication for a small piece of cheese. The expressions on their faces reminded Jamie of soulful puppies. Once he had been like that, begging for every scrap.

"No money, no cheese," a gruff voice called out. "Get, or I'll bring the bobbies down on yer head to cart you to the pauper's prison."

Fearful, the boys started to run away, but Jamie blocked their escape. Reaching into his pocket he took out his last few pennies and placed one in each of the boys' hands. "Here, take these. You need them far more than I." Strange, Jamie thought, how much better it felt to give than to take.

"God bless ye." The boys' eyes shown with gratitude.

"Thankee, guvner."

Thrusting his hands into his pockets, Jamie smiled sadly at the boys, then, still keeping to the shadows, trudged along the cobbled street. Slowly his thoughts gained coherence as he sorted out his emotions. It was as plain as the nose on his face. He cared much more than he should for Catherine Claremont. He was happy just being near her. He was eager to hear the sound of her voice. Just looking at her made him smile. Oh, yes he cared all right. How was he going to stop caring?

Jamie didn't know what possessed him, but suddenly he found himself walking up the steps to Catherine's house. Though for the moment his arm seemed to belong to someone else, he listened as his fist began knocking.

To his surprise, Catherine herself answered the door. He eyed her up and down, wondering why she was wearing a mobcap and why she had a broom in her hands.

"Jamie!"

He tried hard to smile, but all he could manage was a grimace. "Good evening. I hope you are pleasantly surprised."

She was surprised *and* dismayed to find him standing at her door. Self-consciously she touched the cap, all the while hiding the broom behind her back, wondering how she was going to explain.

"Servants' night off?"

Beth's heart did a somersault in her chest. "Yes . . . yes, that's it."

He touched her gently on the tip of her nose with his index finger, then hung his head. "You're a strange one, Catherine. Strange and wonderful and I hope, forgiving."

"Forgiving?" Beth eyed him warily.

Jamie read the question in her eyes. "We must talk."

"Talk?" He wore a black frock coat. His white shirt was open at the neck, revealing the hair on his chest. The tight gray trousers that clung to his body like a second skin emphasized his muscular body. The memory of his lips molded to hers came unbidden to her mind.

"Is there somewhere that we might be alone?" Jamie eyed the stairs.

Bemoaning her lack of privacy, Beth thought quickly. "The carriage house," she answered. It was just far enough away from the house to offer seclusion.

Jamie exhibited the exuberance of a little boy as he bounded into the carriage house and lit the lamp. His breath caught sharply in his throat. She was so lovely, he mused, his eyes moving tenderly over her face, her generous mouth, her neck and the sweet curves that tempted him so.

Jamie came bluntly to the point. It was now or never. "I know we haven't known each other long but Catherine . . . Catherine . . . I want you to marry me."

Oh, how he wanted to feel her nestled in his arms. His gaze slid slowly, lingeringly over her body, touching on her full bosom and he felt his desire stir. It would be a test of his will power if he could be alone with her like this.

"What?" She stiffened, not wanting to go through with her confession now that he was here, now that he had proposed. How could she? And yet, she had to. Otherwise, there was no chance for the future.

"I said, I want you to marry me, Catherine."

Quickly, she plunged ahead. "I'm not . . . not Catherine Claremont," she began.

"What?" Had she learned his secret and was she making fun of him? "Who are you then, the Queen of England?" He laughed.

Suddenly she felt so awkward, so silly. "My name is Beth Longley. I live here with Catherine Claremont."

He realized that she was dead serious. "You're not Catherine Claremont?"

"No, I'm not. You . . . you assumed . . ."

He repeated the name she had revealed. "Beth. Elizabeth. Longley is it?" Oh well, what did it matter? He had seen the clothes she wore, had seen her riding in a fine carriage. What was in a name? "Catherine, Elizabeth, what does it matter?"

"I'm . . . I'm Mrs. Claremont's companion."

He didn't seem to care. Before she could mutter a protest he had one arm around her waist and the other lightly grasping her hand. She was familiar with the sensation of being small and fragile when she was in his arms. Jamie made her feel very, very feminine.

"From the first time I saw you I knew that I wanted you. Not for an hour, not for a day, but forever."

She nestled against him. "Oh, Jamie . . ."

The light in the carriage room was dim. Beth was overwhelmingly conscious of how alone they were.

He stared into her eyes for a long, long time, his gaze softening as he looked at her. "Whoever you are or whatever your name is, you're a lovely woman," he whispered huskily. "Very lovely. I want you to share my life. Will you?"

Beth could feel a blush heating the skin of her face, rising from her chin to forehead. Before she could even think twice, his head had dipped down. His mouth, warm and hard, touched the soft, bare curve of her shoulder igniting a hundred sparks that pulsated through her body.

"Beth. My Beth."

She loved the way he said her name. "I *will* marry you, Jamie," she answered.

"Then I am the world's happiest man." He thought a moment. If it was the time for truth then he had to speak. "I have a confession."

She smiled, thankful that he had made her feel so comfortable with the truth. She would be understanding as well. "You're not really named Jamie?"

He shrugged. "Oh, Jamie is my name, all right. It's just . . . just that I don't have a penny to my name." When she didn't seem to react he was blunt about the truth of it. "I am a pauper. Poor and penniless."

Beth stiffened. He was teasing her, testing her. "No!"

"Ah, but I am!" He affected a jaunty air to hide the apprehension he suddenly felt. "But that won't matter. We can live on *your* money." Now that they were together it all seemed so simple.

"Money?" She shook her head. "I haven't any!"

"What?" He shook his head. "But your clothes!"

Beth took a deep breath. "Mrs. Claremont has been very kind. She allows me to ride in her carriage, live in her house, and she has given me beautiful things to wear. But I have no money to speak of." Sadly, she told him about her father and the last few years of her life on the streets.

Listening, Jamie felt as if all his hopes and dreams were crumbling. They were both playing a masquerade of sorts. It had been nothing but a ghastly hoax, a bizarre twist of fate.

"You!" His disappointment turned to anger, an anger that he turned on her. "You let me think, you let me dream!" Why, she was no better than Annie—a scheming little spider who had woven a silken web around him until his heart was hopelessly in thrall.

"Me!" That he would even fling such an accusation at her was infuriating, particularly under the circumstances. " 'Twas you who sought me out, at the opera, *if* you remember."

His face burned with the truth of her accusation. He had instigated a meeting, but that was because he had thought her to be somebody else. A simple case of mistaken identity that had been magnified by unforeseen circumstances. Still, he couldn't admit his perfidy, even to himself.

"I came to your side, aye. But 'twas you who asked me to dinner, *if you remember!*"

"You didn't have to accept," Beth countered. This wasn't the man who had charmed her the past few days. This man was a stranger. Because it had all been an act, a cruel, devious kind of game. Oh, it was all too clear to her now.

"But you did accept and do you know why?" She spit the words out. "Because you are a fortune hunter. A man who would live upon a woman's money!"

Coming from her it sounded loathsome. "And what is . . . is wrong with that? In London each and every fine citizen lives like a maggot upon the back of someone or other!"

"Oh!" She nearly choked with indignation. How could he so coldly justify his treachery? Without even thinking, she slapped him hard across the face. The sound of her palm striking his cheek reverberated through the quiet of the room like a shot.

An ominous silence fell as they stared at each other for a long, aching moment, each reliving the magic of the past few days. The romance was over before it had even begun. How had it all come to this sad end?

Jamie felt shamed, even more so as he looked at her face. She had such expressive blue eyes that now revealed her pain. Her mouth was tight and quivering. How could he have blamed *her* even for a minute? It was he who had begun this masquerade, purposefully and calculatingly. She *was* innocent, a truth that he now put into words.

"You're right. I am a fortune hunter. You are in no way to blame for any of this." In frustration he threw up his hands. "It was just . . . just that somehow it seemed such a golden opportunity. Turn myself into a replica of a gentleman and marry wealth. Women do it all the time."

"That doesn't make it right," she replied.

"No, it doesn't." His pulse beat violently in his throat as he shook his head. "But maybe if you knew what it had been like for me, perhaps you might understand."

Briefly, yet as impassioned as he could, he told her about his mother's death, his days at the orphanage, ending with his life among London's thieves. "It was either that or starve. Certainly the men and women of the upper class showed me little pity. Not one crust of bread, not even a measure of kindness. The only way I was able to survive at all was because of this!" He tapped his temple. "My wits and my cunning."

"So you were orphaned." Beth's anger was slowly melting. Having witnessed firsthand what went on in London, she couldn't help but have sympathy for him. It was a cruel, uncaring world. He was right. There was no such thing as charity or kindness out on the streets. It was much like a war. The strong survived and the weak died. She thought about Ruth and the others.

"Aye, after me mum died." He quickly looked away so that she wouldn't realize his eyes were misting with tears, not for himself but for his mother and the sadness of her fate.

"Me too . . ."

"You?" Feeling compassion, he gathered her into his arms. Oh, she smelled so good. "Tell me!"

Taking a deep breath, Beth poured out her heart and soul. "My father married a very selfish woman after my mother died. She took him down the path of ruin. He died and I was left all alone. Like you, I had to fend for myself, selling flowers so that I would have enough to eat and a bed, lumpy though it be."

Now he remembered her. "You're the girl. The flower seller in the mobcap." He ran his fingers through her hair as it all came back to him. "I thought you to be so beautiful . . ."

Now Beth remembered, too. "The money pouch! You stole that man's wallet and threw it at me. You nearly got me in trouble and yet . . ." He had inspired special feelings—feelings that had now magnified into what she knew to be the real thing. Love. Despite what Jamie had done or tried to do, she knew without a doubt that she loved him.

"We're two London sparrows!" Jamie whispered against her hair. "Two children of the streets. Each of us seeking to escape our bleak circumstances, albeit in different ways." He kissed her forehead. "You by seeking a more honest means, however."

Who was she to judge him. "I shouldn't have slapped you."

He stiffened. "Ah, but you should have. I deserved it. I have done many things of which I am not proud." He gripped her shoulders. "But know this, Beth Longley, I never lied about my feelings. That, at least, is the truth. I love you!"

"And I you!"

"I'm not the kind of man you need." It was a sad admission. He loved her and yet he didn't have a thing that he could offer her. He was poor! A man with little hope for a future of any kind.

She felt sad for him, even worse with the thought that he might lose faith in himself. "Oh, but you are the kind of man I need. I sense that there is a great deal of love inside of you, a love you once gave to your mother."

"Ah, yes. Me mum." He shook his head. "Wouldn't she be proud if she could see me now."

"Yes, I think she would be."

"But proud of a thief?"

"Proud of the man who wanted more out of life than he had."

"A fortune hunter!" Now that he had been confronted with his motives he loathed himself.

"A man who learned how to speak correctly, walk correctly, and dress like a gentleman. There is nothing wrong with that."

"There is!" Suddenly he pushed away from her. "You deserve better." He turned his head. "Goodbye, Elizabeth! I wish . . ."

The thought of him carrying out his words, of leaving, instilled her with an aching emptiness. She couldn't bear the thought of life returning to the way it was. She had been so lonely. "No, don't leave."

He stared at her a for long, taut moment. His voice was so gentle that she shivered. "I've lived a hard life. I'm no saint. I've stolen and lied but worse yet I made it all right in my own mind. I wish . . ."

"I don't care!" She wanted him just the way he was.

"Maybe not now, but you would. There would come a time when you lost your looks because you had to work so hard, when your smiles turned to frowns and your innocence turned to a hardness of heart. You'd come to hate me some day when the pink clouds blew away and you saw your life with me for what it was." She'd end up just like his mother. He didn't want that.

"Jamie!" She moved toward him, reaching for his hand. "Please, don't leave. Not now."

"Oh God!" He shuddered. He looked deep into her eyes. "I must."

"Why?"

He was blatantly truthful. "Because I. . . . I want you . . ."

Her lashes dropped to veil her eyes. "Oh!"

"I've held myself back because I know the kind of woman you are. The kind of woman a man marries. But I'm a man with hungers."

"Jamie!"

He pulled her so close that there was hardly an inch of their bodies that wasn't touching. A mixture of alarm and pleasure sang inside her veins. "I want to strip off your clothing slowly, sensuously, like petals off a flower and see what lies beneath. I want to cup your breasts in my hands and caress them until . . ." He stepped away. "I want to feel your legs wrapped around my waist, want every inch of our naked flesh to mingle in one long caress. I want all that but I won't touch you. I *won't!*"

Beth was trembling from head to foot. The way he was talking should have embarrassed her, should have made her feel frightened, but strangely enough his words had just the opposite effect. Her body was alive, aching for him to do exactly what he talked about.

"Not even if I want you, too!" She wanted to give him her heart and her soul, and with it, the soft, burning passion of her body. Perhaps their lovemaking could be a healing thing.

A tight ball of pain coiled within Jamie's chest. "You don't know what you want!"

"Oh, but I do!" Her palms pressed against his chest, sliding up to his shoulders. "I want you." She put her arms around his neck. Standing on tiptoe she pressed her slim body to his, holding him. If she clung to him he couldn't go.

"Oh, Beth!" He was crazy about her all right. Dangerously so. His lips were everywhere—her cheeks, her earlobes, her neck, then back to her mouth, his tongue plunging deeply, insistently between her lips.

She felt weak. Shivery. Her fingers clenched his shoulder for fear of falling. "Make love to me . . ."

Her voice caressed his body, touching every nerve. "Where?" Hiding the depth of his feelings he resorted to sarcasm. "In the carriage? On the floor?" He felt stung by the hopelessness of the situation. "I have nowhere to take you, Elizabeth."

"There's my room. Mrs. Claremont has gone with one of her friends to the country. She returns tomorrow morning. Except for Michaels, the house is empty."

"Your room." Oh, how tempting it was and yet, he was determined to protect her.

She glanced toward the house, then back at him. Their eyes met and her heart began to hammer wildly. She loved him. All she knew was that without him she didn't stand a chance of being happy.

Thirteen

Wisps of flickering lamplight danced over the quilt of the bed as if beckoning the two lovers. Yet Jamie didn't hurry. He wanted to take this slow and easy, wanted to be gentle with her.

"Beth!"

For a long heart-wrenching moment Jamie looked deeply into her eyes, then slowly he lowered his mouth to hers, fusing their lips together in a kiss that left her breathless.

Beth's mouth opened to him, her lips trembling. This was what she wanted, to be loved by him. It couldn't be wrong! Not anything that made her feel this way. Closing her eyes, she pressed close to him, her lips parting as she realized the depth of her own need.

Shyly at first, then with increasing boldness, Beth kissed Jamie back with all the hunger in her soul, her tongue moving to meet his. She loved the taste of him, the feel of his passion. Following his lead, she kissed him deeply, her exploring tongue mimicking his. Slowly her arms crept around his neck, her fingers tangling in his thick dark brown hair.

Without disrupting their kiss, Jamie slowly lowered Beth to the bed, then took his place beside her. Gently, he pulled her down until they were lying side by side, his muscled length straining against her softness. He cherished her in deep searching kisses. With trembling fingers he unlaced her bodice, pulling it down around her shoulders, seeking her naked breasts.

"God, you're beautiful!" Jamie had been with many women but Beth's beauty and innocence touched his heart. She was as soft and as delicate as a rose yet he knew her strength and determination. She too had lived upon the streets, but she had made it. She was a lady. A special lady. He wanted to make this beautiful for her, something to remember.

Slowly her shyness thawed. "Am I beautiful, Jamie?" She wanted him to think so.

She heard the soft rhythm of his breath as he spread her hair in a dark cloak about her shoulders.

"Aye. Beautiful. So bloody lovely." Pushing her onto her back he slid his hands down her throat, across her chest, to the breasts he had bared in light circular motions of adoration. "Just about the most beautiful sight any man could behold!"

"Beautiful," she thought. The way he said it made her *feel* beautiful. "Jamie . . ." She spoke his name against his mouth.

As his hands outlined the swell of her breasts, she sank into the softness of the feather mattress. She was aware vaguely of where she was. Her room. And then she put everything else out of her mind as she became aware only of Jamie and what he was doing.

"So much wasted time," he murmured. "But now I'll make up for it."

His head was bent low, his tongue curling around the tips of her breast, suckling gently. She gave a breathless murmur of surprise and her body flamed with desire. She ached to be naked against him. Did that make her a wanton? Then so be it.

Jamie breathed deeply, savoring the rose scent of her perfume. The enticing fragrance invaded his flaring nostrils, engulfing him. "Beth . . . my lovely Beth." Her name was a prayer on his lips. She was the answer to his loneliness and yet she was his pain. He wanted to give her so much and yet he had so little—his heart, his love, himself.

Raising himself up on his elbow he looked down at her and at that moment he knew he'd put his heart and soul in pawn forever. Removing his shirt, he pressed their naked chests together, shivering at the sensation that sent a flash of quicksilver through his veins.

With infinite slowness he continued to undress her, taking the
deepest pleasure in looking at the smooth, creamy flesh that he
had exposed, the firm breasts jutting proudly under his gaze, the
deep coral peaks full and erect. Her waist was just as slim as he
had imagined, her legs just as long and shapely.

His fingers lingered as they wandered down her stomach to
explore the texture of her skin. Like velvet. He sought the inden-
tation of her navel, then moved lower to tangle his fingers in the
soft wisps of hair that joined at her legs. Gently, reverently, he
touched that part of her that had never before been touched by
a man.

"Beautiful and so damned sweet."

Taking off her shoes and stockings he saw that even her feet
were pretty. Slowly, his eyes swept up and down and back again.
He lay looking at her for what seemed to be an eternity, letting
out his breath in an audible sigh.

Beth watched the expressions that moved across his face and
felt a hot ache of desire coil deep within her. "Jamie . . . oh,
Jamie!"

For a long, long while they lay entwined, contenting themselves just in kissing and caressing. Beth relished the yielding
softness of the bed, the velvety coverlet beneath her, warm and
sensuous against her bare shoulders. But most of all, she gave
herself up to the sensations Jamie was creating with his questing
hands, kneading the soft skin of her breasts, teasing the very tips
until his touch made her tremble. An ache was building deep
within her, becoming more and more intense as his fingers fon-
dled and stroked.

Jamie lay stretched out, every muscle in his body taut with
expectation. The tight fabric of his trousers couldn't conceal his
arousal, nor did he seek to hide it from Beth's searching gaze.
Taking her hand he pressed it to the firm flesh. She felt the throb-
bing strength of him as her eyes gazed into his. He bent to kiss
her, his mouth keeping hers a willing captive for a long time.

The warmth and heat of his lips, and the delicate touch of her
fingers on that private part of him sent a sweet ache flaring

through Beth's whole body. Growing bold, she allowed her hands to explore, to delight at the touch of the firm flesh that covered his ribs, his broad shoulders, the muscles of his arms, the lean length of his back. With a soft sigh her fingers curled in the thick, springy hair that furred his chest.

Feeling encumbered by his clothes, Jamie quickly pulled them off and flung them aside. His eyes never left her face as he tossed his boots to the side with a thump. Standing up, he unfolded his tall, muscular frame.

She didn't have time to close her eyes or even to blink before the full glory of his maleness was presented to her. And a glory he was. Beautiful for a man. His shoulders were broad, his chest perfectly formed with a dark mat of hair that seemed to beckon her touch. Her eyes traced the line of his hipbones, then ran down the length of his well-muscled thighs and back again. But it was what lay between his legs that stunned her. He was so perfectly formed.

"I know what you're thinking and I won't!" Jamie whispered huskily.

"Won't what?" Realizing how she was staring, Beth tightly closed her eyes.

"Won't hurt you. I'd never do that, Beth." With a low groan he came to her. "Oh, Darling . . . ! Don't be afraid of me." As if to give her reassurance, he gathered her into his arms, then his mouth covered hers in fierce possession. It seemed he enjoyed kissing and so did she, so very much.

Their bodies touched in an even more intimate embrace. He was aching to possess her and yet he didn't, he took his time, lost in this world of sensual delight. She was in his arms. It was where she belonged. She was his, he would never let her go. Not now.

"Oh, my darling . . . my love . . ."

Beth gloried in the closeness of their bodies, her palms sliding over his muscles and tight flesh to know his body as well as he knew hers. He had said that she was beautiful and yet so was he. He reminded her of a stallion she had seen at the fair—sleek and trim and magnificent. Being so close to him made her feel alive. She trembled in his arms, her whole body quaking as she wondered about what was to follow. She moved against him in a manner that wrenched a groan from his lips.

"Beth. Oh, what you do to me." She could feel exactly what he meant as that certain part of him stiffened even more perceptibly. Like a fire, his lips burned over her. He teased her breasts with a devilish tongue turning her insides molten, her body liquid with the flow of desire.

Moving his hand down her belly he once more touched the soft hair between her thighs, smiling as his fingers came away with a wetness he recognized. Tremors shot through him in fierce waves. He lifted his hips, his hand burrowing between their bodies to guide himself into her.

"Jamie . . ."

His kisses stopped any further words she might have uttered. She felt his maleness at the fragile entryway to her womanhood as he pierced that delicate membrane with a sudden thrust. For one brief moment there was pain, but then Beth's passion rallied. So this was why Ruth and the others cried out so in the night. Wanting to relish this new feeling she pushed upward.

She was so warm, so tight around him that Jamie closed his eyes with agonized pleasure as he slid within her. Burying his length deeply, he moved with infinite care, not wanting to hurt her, instead initiating her fully into the depths of passion. And love.

Tightening her thighs around his waist, Beth arched up to him with sensual urgency. She was melting inside, merging with him into one being. His lovemaking was like nothing she could ever have imagined, filling her, flooding her. Clinging to him, she called out his name.

Jamie groaned as he felt the exquisite sensation of her warm flesh sheathing the long length of him. He possessed her again and again. And yet somehow he couldn't get enough of her. It was as if he wanted to bury himself so deeply inside her that they would be permanently part of each other. His deep moans of pleasure filled the room.

Beth couldn't hold back the whimper that escaped her lips. There was nothing compared to the intense pleasure of being filled by him, loved by him. A wave of sensation rose within her body, her chaste body that hadn't known a man's passion. Her lips parted with each escaping breath.

"No. Don't stop!" she cried out. She knew she would die if he left her now. But he didn't pull away. As she clung to him he moved back and forth in a manner that nearly drove her crazy. Spasms of exquisite feeling flowed through her like a dance, like a roaring wind, like the ocean's tide. She arched her hips hungrily, blending with him. In his arms she wasn't the demure, well-mannered Beth Longley, but a wild thing. Clutching at him, she called out his name, clinging to him with desperate hands. An aching sweetness became a shattering explosion, an escape into a timeless, measureless pleasure.

In the silent aftermath of passion they lay together. Gradually their bodies cooled, their pulses slowed down to a normal rate. "Are you all right, my love?" Jamie was all tender concern for her.

"Yes . . . Yes, I am," she answered shakily. She tightened her arms and her body, holding him inside the warmth of her embrace. For a long, long time they held each other, without speaking. There was no need for words.

Jamie gazed down at her face, gently brushing back the tangled auburn hair from her eyes. "Sleep now," he whispered, still holding her close. With a sigh, she snuggled up against him, burying her face in the warmth of his chest. She didn't want to sleep, not now. She wanted to savor this moment of joy, but as he caressed her back, tracing his fingers along her neck, she drifted off.

For a long, long while Jamie watched her as she slept. He cuddled her against him. She would never know the feelings she inspired. "Dear God!" He hoped with all his heart that she would never regret what had passed between them. The devil damn him for a bastard if he broke her heart. And yet there might come a time when he would have to go. What then?

It was dark in the room. Suffocatingly quiet. Jamie and Beth did not speak, for neither really knew what to say. They had been swept away on a tide of longing for each other that neither could deny. Where were they to go from here?

I love her, Jamie thought, but could he really forget what had happened in the past, what he had once been, could he allow himself a chance to make her happy?

Clasping her arms around her body, Beth was deep in thought, too—remembering every touch, every kiss and caress. Their being together had been the most beautiful moment of her life. A mindless delight of the senses and the heart. Now she wanted to be with him forever. To walk beside him, share in his dreams. When he had entered her she had felt her heart move, had been full of him, full of love. She was richest woman in the world. But what of Jamie? What was he thinking now?

Jamie's thoughts were as potent as Beth's. He closed his eyes, remembering. Never had he realized that love could be like this. And yet what to do about it? Marriage? It was out of the question now. He had nothing to offer Beth. And yet, he wanted to give her the world.

He was dressed only in his breeches. No shirt, no shoes. The thought that he could so easily divest himself of his trousers and crawl into bed with her again kept tugging at his brain. At this moment that was what he really wanted and yet he held himself back.

He sprawled in his chair, stretching his long legs out in front of him as he thought things out. He could nearly imagine what a beautiful child she must have been, orphaned and walking the streets just as he had. Only Beth hadn't resorted to the kind of life that he had. Was that because she was more noble than he?

"Bloody damn! Bloody damn!" he swore. Why was it she made him feel so guilty?

"Beth, are you awake?" There was an edge to his voice that he tried to temper. A frustration with himself.

"Yes. I never went to sleep. I couldn't."

He suddenly felt the need to talk, to make her understand. "I would never go back to a life of thieving. I was miserably unhappy, only I didn't know it then."

"I know. I could see it in your eyes." There was a pause. "Jamie . . ." She loved him, there was no doubt or question in her mind as to that. Her senses were filled with wanting him. "Then go to him," a voice inside her head whispered. Life was all too short, so uncertain. One never knew what the future held in store. But he was here with her now and she wanted him to make love to her again. If he couldn't make any promises, well, so be it.

Rising from the bed, Beth padded across the hard wooden floor on bare feet. Leaning toward him she stroked his neck, tangling her fingers in his hair. Jamie closed his eyes, giving himself up to the rippling pleasure.

"Make love to me again . . ." She leaned forward to brush his mouth with her lips. That simple gesture said all she wanted to say, that she loved him, that she desired him. Slowly, his hands closed around her shoulders, pulling her to him, answering her shy kiss with a passion that made her gasp. Gathering her into his arms, he carried her back to the bed.

"I'm only human . . . and I do want you. So very much." His hands roamed gently over her body, lingering on the fullness of her ripe breasts, leaving no part of her free from his touch.

She gave herself up to the fierce emotions that raced through her, answering his touch with searching hands, returning his caresses. Closing her arms around his neck, she offered herself to him, writhing against him. She could feel the pulsating hardness of him through the fabric of his trousers and reached up to pull his breeches from him.

Sweet hot desire fused their bodies together as he leaned against her. His strength mingled with her softness, his hands moving up her sides, warming her with his heat. Like a fire, his lips burned a path from one breast to the other, bringing forth spirals of pulsating sensations that swept over her like a storm.

Jamie's mouth fused with hers, his kiss deepening as his touch grew bolder. Beth luxuriated in the pleasure of his lovemaking, stroking and kissing him back. He slid his hands between their bodies, poised above her. The tip of his maleness pressed against her, entered her softness in a slow but strong thrust, joining her in that most intimate of embraces.

He kissed her as he fused their two naked bodies together and from the depths of her soul, her heart cried out. It was a tiny flicker of hope that all was not lost, that somehow they would find a way.

A flame of yearning that he would come to trust her, care for her, surged through her as he whispered her name. Tightening her thighs around his waist, she wanted him to move within her. He did, slowly at first, then with a sensual urgency.

Jamie filled her with his love, leaving her breathless. It was like falling from a cloud—falling and never quite hitting the ground. Her arms locked around him as she arched to meet his body in a sensuous dance; forgetting all her inhibitions as she expressed her love. A sensation burst through her, a warm explosion.

Even when the sensual magic was over they clung to each other, unwilling to let the moment end. Beth was reluctant to have him leave her body, felt that surely the fire they had ignited tonight would meld them together for eternity. Smiling, she lay curled in the crook of Jamie's arm, and he, his passion spent, lay close against her, his body pressing against hers. They were together. It was all she had for now. For the moment it had to be enough.

Only when she was fast asleep did Jamie get up. Slowly disentangling himself from her arms, he rose from the bed and moved about the room, gathering up his clothes. He had to get out of here now, had to think. There were so many changes in his life that needed to be dealt with. A long walk in the night air would aid him immensely.

* * *

Soft rays of sunlight fluttered through an opening in the curtains. From beneath the window the sound of Londoners going about their daily routine at last pierced through the fog of Beth's dreams.

"Mmmm . . ." Hugging her body, she nestled herself in a heap of blankets remembering the night before.

Lover. Once Beth might have thought the word to have a tawdry ring to it, but feeling as she did about Jamie she couldn't believe that the pleasure they found together was wrong. He had known just how to touch her, the right words to say, how long to caress her, how to bring her again and again to a crest of pleasure.

Once she might have blushed at the thought of a man learning every inch of her body, yet with Jamie it just seemed as natural as breathing. She had given herself to him without reserve, looking forward to the rest of their lives together.

"Jamie . . ." Just the whisper of his name on her lips made her heart sing. She gave to him her whole heart because she was incapable of holding the tide of her feelings in reserve. She granted him all her love, her strength, her devotion because it was not in her nature to give him less.

He had known coldness, hardship, and pain before building that thick wall of bravado around himself. Sometimes to stay alive, he had been forced to live by his wits and his strength. Beth wanted to heal him with tenderness and the soft, burning, worship of her body. She wanted to protect him, to keep him safe.

"But how?"

Beth rolled to the edge of the bed. Bending over, she picked up her clothes, scattered about the hard wooden floor where Jamie had left them. Slipping into her chemise and petticoat she pulled the drawstring at the waist allowing herself to dream. Beth Morgan! The two names fit so perfectly together. Would it ever be? Would Jamie ever be in a position to marry her? Perhaps, if she helped him turn his life around.

"I'll talk to Mrs. Claremont. She'll help me!" Wouldn't she? Beth could only hope that she would. Catherine had wanted her to find love and a man who would take care of her. Somehow she would have to make her realize that despite his circumstances, Jamie Morgan was that man.

She smiled. After all, hadn't it been Catherine Claremont who had instigated this entire thing? It had been. Although Catherine had thought Jamie to be her friend's son, everything had turned out just as it should.

"I'll talk to her at breakfast!" Beth had decided to tell Catherine everything about Jamie. Today. This morning. She would try to portray it in a humorous light, like an opera or a play. Dressing in a blue and green plaid wool dress that reminded her of a tartan, she thought about what she would say. Soundlessly, she opened the door and stepped out into the hall, then closed the door behind her. It was then that she heard the soft tapping at the front door.

Beth waited. When no one else answered the door, she did. "Jamie!"

"It was cold outside."

It was. A brisk wind whipped at Beth's hair as she stood in the doorway.

Beth threw her arms around him. "What a pleasant surprise!"

"I just came by to tell you that I did it! I left Annie and the thieves. I may be poor, but from now on at least I'll be an honest bloke." Bending his head he kissed her for a long time. At last he pulled away. "It is going to be hard. But I'm willing to do what I must. I saw a sign in the clockmaker's window. The owner is in need of a man to keep his ledgers." He shook his bead. "I don't know . . ."

"I've worked with ledgers. I'll help you!" She opened the door wide and beckoned him inside. "Together we can do anything, Jamie."

He smiled at the word "together." "By God, I think we can."

"Jamie . . ." She worried about him. "Do you have some place to stay?"

He shook his head. "No, not yet."

"I'll talk to Mrs. Claremont and see if perhaps you could stay for awhile in the carriage house. It's warm and there is a settee in there that you could use for a bed." Impetuously, she reached out for him, her hand resting on the firm hardness of his chest. "Oh, Jamie. It will all work out. I know it. You did the right thing!" Standing on tiptoe, her eyes riveted on his mouth, she initiated a kiss.

"Mmmmm," he groaned, pulling her into his arms. A hungry desire that clamored for release, swept through his body as he caressed her lips. His mouth closed on hers, engulfing her in a maelstrom of delicious sensations.

Passionately, Beth yielded to him as her lips and teeth parted to allow his exploration. Her hands slid up to lock around his neck, her fingers tangling in the thickness of his dark hair. She sighed against his mouth, trembling with pleasure. This, this was what she had wanted to experience again, to be in his arms and have him kiss her.

The feel of him, strong, warm, and loving was all Beth wanted in the world. She didn't fully understand everything that was happening to her, she only knew that he alone could arouse such an urgent need within her. He was the source of every comfort, every beautiful thing she could imagine at this moment.

Jamie forgot everything but the sweet, soft lips beneath his. He was aware of nothing but an intense driving need for her. Tightening his arms around her, his kiss deepened in intensity as he explored the moist sweetness of her mouth, craving her kiss as others might crave brandy. He didn't know why he had come, only that he was here.

Jamie inhaled her fragrance. Roses. A sweet aroma. Desire bubbled like a powerful tide, hot and sweet as he continued to kiss her. He had always kept a cool head in matters of the heart, but whenever she was near he was totally at the mercy of his emotions. It was only by the greatest self-control, as a matter of fact, that he was at last able to pull away.

"Mrs. Claremont might see," he whispered. "But I do want to see you tonight."

"Tonight?"

His hand crept up the wool covering her rib cage to close over the shapely curve of her breast. "Mmmmm," he whispered. "I hope that is soon enough." He grinned. "Tonight!"

Quickly, Beth kissed him goodbye. Closing the door, she tried to calm her breathing.

"Miss Beth!" Michaels's voice startled her as he came up behind her.

"Good morning!" She felt so happy that impulsively she kissed him on the cheek. "Where is Catherine! I hope she's not impatient with me for being late to breakfast again but I have to talk to her. I have to tell her something very important."

"Miss Beth." The grim expression on the butler's face alarmed Beth. "What is it?"

"It's Mrs. Claremont."

"Catherine!" Dear God, something had happened.

"There was a carriage accident."

"An accident!" Beth was stunned.

"The roads were slick as they often are in winter. The carriage hit a wagon while on a country road headed back toward London." Michaels's voice was choked. "Catherine was somehow thrown out. She . . . she hit her head."

"Oh, no!" Hurrying to the hall closet she tugged at her cloak. "Where is she? I must go to her. She'll need me to help her while she gets well. She . . ."

Michaels put his hand on her arm. "My dear . . . Mrs. Claremont is . . . is dead!"

"Dead?" Beth gasped. "No, it can't be true. Not Catherine. She was so full of life." She closed her eyes, fighting back tears as she remember the woman's advice. "Life is very short and unpredictable when all is said and done. A person, man or woman, should live it to the fullest. Each and every minute of every day. For one never knows . . ."

"Dead!" Her face was wet with tears.

* * *

The tick of the clock on the bedside table marked off the minutes as Beth tried to realize what had occurred. Be happy, Catherine had said. How could she be happy? She had no one in the world to turn to now. Except Jamie.

Where would she go? Mrs. Claremont had a nephew she had termed a "wastrel." He would inherit everything now. He would turn Beth out. Suddenly, the bright embers of her world had turned to ash and she couldn't help wondering what was to become of her.

Jamie smiled as he tore up the clockmaker's sign and threw it away. He started work tomorrow. The hours were from six in the morning until eight at night. More importantly, the clockmaker, a jovial old fellow, had also given him a room at the back of the store with a bed and desk. Now Jamie could keep his pride and not have to live on Catherine Claremont's charity.

He whistled happily as he strode down the street. If he had only realized earlier how truly good it felt to be honorable he would have done it far sooner. Just wait until he told Beth. He'd have to wait until tonight.

"No, not tonight." He wanted to see her now, at this very minute.

Strange. A sudden sense of impending danger swept over him, though why Jamie couldn't say. With a shrug he kept walking. Still, he looked cautiously over his shoulder, stealing a quick glance up and down the labyrinth of merging roads. A familiar face appeared from the shadows, startling him.

Jamie recognized him at once. He was one of the judges Annie sometimes bribed.

Slumping against the brick wall, he instinctively tried to hide, then shrugged his fear away again. He wasn't a thief anymore. "Calm yerself, Jamie ole boy," he advised, listening to himself.

That was why he didn't react, even when he heard the man cry out.

"There he is. After him!"

Jamie stood as if rooted to the cobblestones, watching as other men came out from the dark, pointing their fingers. Then, just in the nick of time, he realized. They *were* chasing him!

"Seize him!"

Jamie turned to flee but the men quickly closed in, cornering him. One had him by the arm. What else could he do but try to reason with them? "What is going on?" he asked.

"Are you Jamie Morgan?"

Once he would have lied through his teeth. Now, however, since his change of heart, he told the truth. "I am!"

"He's a swindler. A thief!"

Jamie stood up straight with pride. "I am not! There must be some mistake. I'm a working man." He tried to appear calm. "I work for Theodore Otis, the clockmaker. If you will just talk to him he will tell you."

"Otis?" For just a moment the man hesitated as if he intended to at least grant Jamie that. A woman stepped out of the shadows at that moment.

Jamie gasped in surprise. "Annie!"

Helpless, he stood there as she ticked off a list of his supposed crimes, some of them her own. The brutal betrayal stung him.

"Annie. Why?"

"Because . . ."

Was there regret in her voice? What did it matter? As Jamie was pushed into a wagon and taken into custody, he feared the worst.

Jamie had said that he was going to see her tonight, yet as the hours ticked by there was no sign of him. Where was he? What could have happened to him to keep him from coming?

Sitting in front of the window, Beth stared forlornly at Catherine's sprawling estate. If ever she had needed him, she needed him now, for Catherine's death had sent her spiraling into the darkest despair. This woman had been more than a companion. In some ways she had been like a mother, always kind, always caring.

"What is going to happen now?" Beth was chilled by her emotions. She had never felt so desolate, so alone. "Oh, Jamie . . ."

What if something had happened to him! The streets held hidden menace. What if a thief or an assailant had caught him unaware? What if someone had robbed the clocksmith's shop and hit him on the head? What if . . .

Jamie had said, that he wanted the job. Perhaps he was working. No doubt at this moment Jamie was bent over his ledgers, unaware of the lateness of the hour.

Tick, tick, tick. The sound of the clock marked off the time. Eight o'clock. Nine. Ten. Eleven. At last, giving up hope that he was going to come, at least tonight, Beth went up to bed.

The ugly gray walls of Newgate loomed before Jamie's eyes. The doors, banded with iron, seemed to grin at him evilly and he shivered. *Newgate!* The name used to chill his blood with dread when he was picking pockets.

"Move along . . . !"

The heavy spiked doors swung open with a groan, then, after he had been pushed inside, clanged shut behind him. What a horrible place, he thought, eyeing the rough, heavy walls. Horrible and deadly.

The stale odor of rotting straw assailed Jamie's nostrils and he flinched. He passed through the doorway and into the depths of the prison. The nauseating stink of Newgate continued to assault him the farther he went, pressing upon him like an enveloping miasma.

"What is that odor?" he asked the guard.

"The smell of death. The inmates call it "Newgate perfume." The hangman leaves his "gibbet fruit," as he calls it, swinging all week before he cuts them down, as a special lesson to those inside here. A way of frightening them into abandoning their life of crime, ye might say."

"Dear God!" Jamie exclaimed. It seemed a most hideous thing to do. He looked over his shoulder as if fearing something or someone might suddenly pop out at him.

The noisy, clamorous, pathetic-looking creatures that shuffled along with a length of chain between their ankles, or hovered behind the grating, striking at the iron bars, made his stomach lurch. It was like glimpsing purgatory. There was a look of hopelessness in the staring eyes that touched his soul.

"Poor souls! Just like me!"

And then it was his turn. Pushed and shoved along the endless corridors, he was forced to descend the steeply winding staircases into a place that reminded him of hell. Even his worst nightmares paled compared to the reality of what he found inside.

As Jamie walked along, his eyes searched in the dim light, staring through the grates. The prisoners' forms were hidden from public view in their cell blocks. All he could see were their clutching hands as the gaolers rationed out their moldy bread and unappetizing food. This was to be his fate.

"Oh, Beth!" He had promised her that he would come tonight. Now he must break that promise. And all because of a woman's jealousy! "Damn you, Annie. Damn you to hell!" He was doomed. Unless . . .

Closing his eyes he thought of Beth. She was his only hope.

Fourteen

It was quiet. Nearly as quiet as the morgue had been when Beth had paid her last respects to the woman who had befriended her. Only the scratching sound of a pen disturbed the silence as the lawyer took down some notes.

"Please be seated." With those words it all began.

Beth clasped her hands tightly together as the solicitor began to read the last will and testament of Catherine Anne Claremont in a low, droning voice. Her baggage was all packed with the few possessions she had brought to the house. She was fully prepared to leave. Ned Pritchart, Catherine Claremont's nephew would own the property now and he planned to sell it quickly to pay his debts. There would be no place for Beth.

"I Catherine Claremont, being of sound mind do heretofore put forth my last will and testimony." The man read, using a string of long difficult words Beth didn't understand.

"The Claremont fortune is rumored to be at least six hundred thousand pounds at the very least," a primly coiffed lady was whispering behind her fan.

"I've heard it is considerably more. Someone will be unreasonably wealthy after today," a bespectacled man answered.

"No doubt her charities, of which she had several," another woman added. "You know how she sympathized with the poor."

"Aye, and I hear she was estranged from her nephew. Surely, however, she wouldn't really carry out her threats to write him out of her will."

"Knowing Catherine I think that she would."

Six hundred thousand pounds, Beth thought. She'd never realized there was so much money in the entire world and yet not even such vast riches had been able to keep Catherine Claremont safe, or bring her back her life. Money could not buy everything!

"To the Sisters of Mercy I bequeath the amount of five hundred pounds annually." All eyes focused on a dark-clothed woman dressed as a nun.

"To Bethlehem Hospital, formerly Bedlam, I leave the sum of six hundred pounds annually with the strict provision that the money be used not for restraining the unfortunates but for aiding them."

"To Christ's Church I bequeath the annual sum of two hundred pounds a year."

"To my widowed brother-in-law I leave two shillings, the exact amount he owned when he married into my family." A muffled oath was heard. Bolting to his feet a tall, skinny man with a long nose protested. He was sternly silenced.

"To my loyal butler, Michaels, I declare Claremont house to be his home as long as he wishes. He may not be cast out. I have set aside a sum that will pay him his regular salary for the rest of his life."

Meeting Michaels's eye, Beth smiled, glad that the man who had been loyal to Catherine would be secure now that she was gone. Perhaps all was not lost. Maybe she too could stay. Maybe the same provision had been made for her—as a maid. Michaels had proven himself to be her friend and had always complimented her on her chores. With a house as large as this there was always work to be done. And yet without Catherine's warm smile it would be a lonely place.

I have to pinch myself to believe that she is really gone, Beth thought with a sigh. And yet, the memory of Catherine Claremont lying so still in the coffin at the funeral was all too real. Ned Pritchart had been lavish in choosing a headstone. A white marble angel with huge wings standing on a globe representing the earth. It was a symbol that the Claremont investments encompassed the world, he had said.

Beth listened as the list of bequeathments went on and on, covering the servants who had been so very loyal to the matron of Claremont House. Strange, she thought, how Ned Pritchart had grieved so little for his aunt. Nor had he made much pretense of remorse that she was now gone. His coldness, in fact, was somehow less than human. Was it greed? Or was there something else bubbling beneath his icy aloofness?

From beneath her lashes she looked Ned's way, not at all surprised to see a pretty young woman sitting by his side. She wondered what they were talking about now as they bent their heads together. Then as she heard a piercing giggle she could only gasp.

"Silence." The solicitor was visibly angered by such little show of respect.

"Silence yourself!" Smugly Ned Pritchart whispered, "Once I latch on to the old witch's fortune I do anything I please." Counting on his fingers he tried to calculate just what net sum he would be granted.

"Ahem . . ." Looking chastisingly over the rim of his spectacles, the solicitor urged him to silence again.

The rest of the will's reading progressed rapidly as each servant was named along with the amount they were to receive. Catherine Claremont was taking care of everyone who had been near and dear to her, seemingly rewarding each according to how they had treated her. Suddenly, however, the tempo slowed. It was obvious that it was coming to an end, and the mood of anticipation heightened. Just how rich would this young man be, all seemed to be wondering.

"To my nephew I leave my Bible in the hope that he will have something to while away the time when he is in debtor's prison. I also leave my small cottage house in Devonshire. Said house may not be sold nor credited to pay any debts. A sum of five thousand pounds is to be used for his education and for that alone. In addition, I leave him a trust fund that shall be strictly administered over a monthly period, to total fifty pounds a month."

"Fifty pounds?" Once again Ned Pritchart bounded to his feet.

" 'Tis a pittance. I'll contest this will. The old woman was crazy! Aye, that's it."

"As crazy as a fox," the solicitor said beneath his breath. He moved on. "The bulk of my estate, including the house I have loved so dearly, my jewels, and a comfortable allowance, I leave to Miss Elizabeth Longley, my companion, friend, and surrogate daughter." Those words were met with an amazed gasp as all eyes turned in Beth's direction.

"What?" Beth didn't realize that she had spoken aloud, but she had.

"To *her?*" Running up to the solicitor, Ned Pritchart banged his fist on the desk. "I protest! I protest! She is no kin of my aunt's." He waved his fist accusingly at Beth, glaring all the while. "There is villainy at work here, Sir. That woman is a fortune hunter and mayhap worse."

"Silence!" The solicitor went on with the terms of the will, verifying that indeed what he had said was correct. Catherine Claremont had been very diligent in making certain the document was quite legal and binding.

Beth sat silent, too stunned to speak. She, once a merchant's daughter, then a flower seller, then a maid, was now just as rich as she had once been poor. But money couldn't buy happiness.

"I've heard no word from Jamie! It was as if he had just disappeared. Where was he? Why hasn't he come?" she thought to herelf. Closing her eyes she concentrated upon his name, as if in that way she could send a silent message to his heart.

It was dark and damp in the windowless cell except for one lone taper whose flame flickered and sparked. Jamie lay rigidly on his side on the hard pallet, his mouth tightened in anger as he watched the glow of the candleflame. He was a prisoner by God. *A prisoner awaiting trial.*

He had wanted to make a change in his life, had wanted to make something of himself. Now the only place his name was recorded was in the large leatherbound prison book. He had been led along the dank dimly lit stone passages. A thick iron-hinged door had swung and he had been pushed into a stinking cell with a small barred window.

He shuddered. Ever since his days at the orphanage when he had been punished by being locked in a linen closet for misbehaving, he had hated closed-in places. And yet there was little he could do.

"I want to get out!"

He had never really appreciated his freedom before; now he did. Even being poor was better than being in this place.

He turned over on his back closing his eyes. Sleep. That's what he wanted, what he needed. There was nothing he could do tonight. He would rest and then in the morning he would come to a decision as to what to do. Surely, there had to be some hope.

He bolted up as something ran across his legs. Rats! He could hear their chatter, see the glow of their eyes. Rats! Living in the Dials, he had seen many. Even so, he hated them.

"Dirty little beggars!" If they were hungry enough they would bite. "Here!" Taking a piece of stale bread left over from supper he tossed it on the floor, wincing as he heard their scamper. "That will keep them occupied for awhile." He watched as two rats fought over the scrap.

Lying on his back, his arms folded, his head resting on his hands he tried to think of a plan to get out. He knew in his heart that it was hopeless. That is unless Annie had a change of heart. Would she? No. Women could be stubborn.

"Damn her. Damn her I say!" he muttered. And damn himself for being such a fool. He shouldn't have told Annie that he was leaving. He should have just disappeared. So much for his sense of friendship and honor. All it had gotten him was a trip to Newgate.

In frustration he sprang from the bed to pace the confines of the small room. And all the while the candle burned down to a nub, at last leaving Jamie in total darkness.

* * *

Jamie stood wearily with ten other unfortunates as he awaited his trial in the courtroom. He had been escorted with several other prisoners past the cells of Newgate, through the yards, and out through the heavily iron-studded door into the waiting prison wagons. There with several other frightened, dirty, and disheveled men and women he had been brought to Old Bailey, the criminal court of London.

The room was filled with noisy, laughing, jeering people who seemed to view the sentencing of miscreants as entertainment. Jostling each other, they fought for seats that would give them a good view of the proceedings. The judge and counsel in their intricately curled white wigs made little effort to keep any semblance of order.

"Trial, they calls it. Ha, I says!" A ragged woman standing next to him snorted her disdain. "Don't know why they bother, I don't. They 'ave already made up their minds. Guilty."

"Aye, of being poor."

"And for that we'll stay here forever."

"If we escape the 'angman. And then again, we might be transported to Australia and go through hell in a convict ship. Is that justice?"

Transported. Jamie clenched his teeth. To him that would be the worst punishment of all, for it would take him far away from Beth. Hopelessly far away.

"Aye to Sydney or New South Wales to work on some plantation until we drop."

"And all on account of five shillings. 'Ats the amount we can be 'anged for stealing. Five lousy shillings!" The man kept muttering this over and over. "Five shillings."

Jamie anxiously scanned the crowd, hoping against hope for any sign of Beth. And yet, why would she even think to see him here? She had no way of knowing that he had been taken in. Worse yet, he had no way of letting her know his fate. As far as she was concerned he had just disappeared.

The proceedings were conducted with calm indifference, as if merely a matter of business. There was a great deal of form, but no compassion, considerable interest, but no sympathy. Jamie watched grimly, assessing the judge who sat pompously straight, the Lord Mayor mimicking an equal measure of dignity, the barrister who seemed anxious for the morning to be over.

The other prisoners were dealt with quickly and efficiently. Three prisoners were condemned to the gallows, two to the pillory, one young lad was given the lesser penalty of the lash. Taking a deep breath Jamie prepared himself for his own ordeal. He was determined to face whatever happened with dignity, to hide his deep all-consuming heartache. Then, suddenly the judge was talking to him.

"What is your name?" The judge eyed him sternly.

"Jamie!"

"Jamie who?"

"Morgan," he said with a sigh, wishing he had brought more honor to it.

The judge looked at him over the rim of his spectacles. "Have you any witnesses to speak to your character?"

Jamie shook his head. "There is one, a young woman. The jailors wouldn't allow me to contact her."

"A young woman. Who?"

Jamie looked down at his hands. It was too late to involve Beth in all of this. Better then, perhaps, that he just let her forget him.

"No witnesses," the judge repeated, nodding to a clerk who scratched the information down on a long roll of paper.

"The charge is stealing. How do you plead?"

"If a man is judged by the present and not by the past I plead not guilty."

The judge raised his brows, obviously annoyed and anxious to get the matter over and done with. "I have a signed affidavit that says you did steal." He quickly ticked off the charges and Jamie was dismayed to find that Annie had accused him of stealing from her. The exact amount of his diction lessons. How ironic! What's more she hadn't even had the courage to face him with her treacherous accusation. She had merely had it written down in a document.

"I don't care what that paper says."

"Hmmmm. He won't confess." The prosecutor shrugged with a sly look in his eyes. "Then I would submit, My Lord, that the prisoner be sent to the ships. A sea voyage might change his attitude."

"Mmmmm. . . ." The judge thought it over. "The cells are overcrowded and the citizens seem to prefer sending our criminals over the sea. There are two ships right now moored in the Thames."

"No!" It was the worst sentence he could have been granted, yet Jamie had no recourse, no say in the matter. He was swept from the dock, taken down the stairs and hustled toward the prison wagon again, the judge's words echoing in his mind.

Fifteen

Rain pattered steadily upon the roof. It was a dismal day. The kind of day that only added to Beth's dismal mood. Jamie had disappeared, or so it seemed. Five days had passed by and still he hadn't come. Why?

"Are you ready for breakfast, Mum?" Peeping through the doorway Sarah made her inquiry.

"Toast and tea." She wasn't very hungry. "And maybe some fruit."

That's all? Why, you'll waste away, Mum."

Beth sighed. "Maybe I will." Worry ate away at her, that, and grief for her friend, Catherine. Nor was she used to the fact that this house belonged to her, at least for now. Ned Pritchart was doing everything within his power to have the will overturned. Storming about, he had threatened to have her thrown out in the street.

"Oh, Jamie, if I ever needed you I need you now." Then why hadn't he come? Was it because of what had happened? Now that she was wealthy in reality did he fear she might think of him as a fortune hunter again? If so, then he was being so very foolish.

No, that isn't it! She felt something else. Something deep inside. She sensed some kind of danger. He had left the thieves. What if they had retaliated against him in some way because of his decision? Beth longed for the womblike comfort of a hot bath.

* * *

The water in the brass tub felt warm and wonderful. Beth lingered in the bath, sponging herself, imagining the cloth to be Jamie's caress. Remembering his love for roses, she reached for a bar of soap that held that fragrance. Leaning back, she closed her eyes and luxuriated in the water, sighing with pleasure as rapture spread through her body.

Stepping from the tub and wrapping herself in a large towel, she dried herself, then set about finding just the right dress to wear. She chose a simple dark green dress of wool with neck just high enough to be decent but low enough to be interesting. Around her neck she tied a ribbon with a cameo that had been one of Catherine's gifts.

Always one to scorn corsets before, Beth had a change of heart, allowing the maid to lace her up tightly. As to her hair, she remembered Jamie asking her about its length and decided to let it just hang free. To make certain the auburn waves were shiny, she brushed it a hundred times. Viewing herself in the mirror she nodded, pleased with her decision of dress and coiffuer. Today was the day she was going to find him, even if she had to go to the Dials to do so.

Taking a woolen wrap from the hall closet, Beth instructed the carriage driver where to go. The Dials. She'd start looking for him there.

"The Dials?" He looked at her as if she had lost her mind.

"Yes, the Dials." It was a bumpy ride to that irregular square into which streets and courts plunged in all directions. They passed by a pawnbroker's shop, secondhand clothing store, two gin shops, and assorted broken-down dwellings, many with rags or papers in the broken windows. A stark contrast to where she lived now. Beth was shocked. How could she have forgotten? Dicing, whoring, and gin drinking were activities pursued here. That and thievery.

"Mmmmm . . . this isn't the place for a lady," the carriage driver said.

"I know . . ." She stuck her head out the window, searching every passerby's face. "Oh, Jamie, where are you?"

"G'daiy, Missie." A grinning, patched and tattered man waved at Beth as she turned the corner, tipping his hat in the manner of a gentleman.

On Impulse Beth had the driver pull over to the curb. She gave the little man a detailed description of Jamie. but he said he hadn't seen him. They moved on to another pedestrian, then another, and another.

"Oh, please. I'm looking for Jamie Morgan," she said. Alas, no one had seen him.

Remembering Jamie's delight at having found a job, she quickly directed the driver to every clock shop in London. Not until the last one, however, did she find out any information.

"Yes, I remember the dark haired gent. I offered him a job and a room out back." The old man sniffed indignantly. "He never showed up."

"What?"

"I haven't heard a word from him, so I hired someone else."

"No!" Beth's breath caught in her throat. Her hands trembled.

Climbing back in the carriage she felt panicked. Something had happened to Jamie yet she didn't know where to start. She didn't know where he had lived, didn't know any of the people he had known. What then?

Scotland Yard, the sign read. It was the home of the detective department of the London police. Beth wasted no time in seeking them out.

"Can I help you, Miss?" A bald man with a thick mustache was quick to offer his assistance. Between puffs upon his pipe, he questioned her as to the reason for her presence in the office

"A . . . a friend of mine has disappeared," she answered, running her fingers through her slightly touseled hair.

"Disappeared. Explain."

Beth did, giving him a vivid description of Jamie, even to the color of his clothing the last time she had seen him. "He told me he was going to see me that night and that was several days ago."

"Mmmmmm." The man's piercing brown eyes scrutinized Beth. "Perhaps there is another woman."

"No!" She shook her head violently. "Something has happened." She took a deep breath then confided, "He had some unsavory friends. The day I saw him he had told them he didn't want to associate with them anymore."

"And you fear foul play."

"I do!"

"Perhaps even murder?"

"No!"

The man took out a pair of spectacles and put them on. "How can you be so sure?"

"Because I think I would feel it, here." She touched her heart.

"I see."

Beth's jaw tightened. "Please, help me."

"Did he ever frequent the docks?" There was insinuation in the man's tone of voice, as if to chide Jamie unfairly for his lack of discretion.

"No! Never. Why?"

"Because a body was found there this morning. I thought . . ."

"Well, you were wrong!" She wouldn't believe Jamie could be dead. In trouble perhaps, but not dead. Beth's patience was waning. She was in a hurry to get this matter settled so she could find Jamie before something sinister happened.

"I can pay your price and I assure you I am most sincere." Taking out her money pouch she hefted it temptingly.

"It's not a matter of money." The man looked insulted. Still he didn't refuse her offer. This time when Beth spoke of her fears the man listened attentively.

"So, he lived among less than respectable citizens. London's underworld, a venomous snake with a hide-away in the dark holes under ground, in hidden back rooms of dirty houses, or on the gloomy banks of the Thames. The women that follow them are in most cases even more devious than the men. Ferocious." He punctuated his sentences by taking a puff on his pipe and blowing the smoke out in a series of small bursts. "Hard to tell what might have happened, but I don't envy him."

Neither did Beth. As she left Scotland Yard she felt strangely unnerved. It was even worse than she had feared.

Thunder boomed and lightning pierced the sky with its fiery ribbon. A furious rainstorm pounded the decks of the Sea Horse, a ship waiting to sail. The prison ship was bound for Australia as soon as the weather cleared.

It was cold. Cold and penetratingly damp. Jamie sat huddled in a corner, shivering as he clutched his tattered cloak. He had given his blanket to a woman more in need of it than he. Besides, what did it matter if he caught a chill? He had little to live for anyway.

"Beth!"

In truth all of his fighting spirit had been taken from him. Without Beth in his life he just didn't care anymore. His eyes held no sparkle, no fire. Hope was something he had long since discarded.

"Beth . . ." he whispered again.

Perhaps not seeing her was a blessing in disguise. He wouldn't want her to see how low he had fallen. And yet, he was not as unfortunate as some. So far he had not succumbed to the fever that had taken others. At least so far he had a measure of health. Some of the others were not so lucky. There was ague, the pox, and constant coughing. A number of the prisoners were disturbed by the constant rocking of the ship and vomited their protest on the straw-covered floor.

Looking through the grille of the wooden door, he could see the shadow of the gaoler coming toward him. "Get back, yer 'ags. Move aside, yer gaping bastards! We got us another thief."

Brutally, a young woman was thrust inside. A sudden shriek-ing, snarling, shouting fight broke out among three of the women over the ownership of a tattered piece of cloth. Each woman claimed it belonged to her. Ignoring the protestations of the real

owner, they clawed, kicked, and lashed out. They professed no
fear of the gaoler as they flew at each other. Still, as the prison
guard put the key in the lock, the prisoners scattered, like cock-
roaches disturbed by a sudden light.

"Is it meal time? Oh, how I relish the gruel yer gi' us."

"Ye'll eat it and like it!" the guard growled testily. He was a
burly man with frizzled brown hair, a bulbous nose, and a per-
petual scowl.

"Mayhap he's going to take us for a walk." The woman who
had stolen the blanket smiled sweetly. "Like the dogs he thinks
we are."

"The only walk ye'll be granted is a hike up the gallow's steps
if ye don't shut yer mouth!"

"Better the gallows than this stinking hole!"

"Then I'll hurry to comply." The guard picked up some rope,
pretending that he was going to hang it from one of the beams.
"I'll 'ang yer. I will!"

"No!"

"I didn't think so." The guard rasped on. "Yer don't know how
lucky yer be that ye've got a fine ship to take ye away. This one
is nearly seaworthy." He guffawed. Hopefully it will get yer to
Botany Bay wi'out sinking. Why, this is a palace compared to
most."

"A palace," Jamie thought. Hardly that. Conditions aboard the
convict hulks were unspeakably horrible, with unwashed criminals, both men and women, packed together closely on all three
decks, breathing permanently fouled air.

Nor was there any hope for escape. There were those prisoners
who espoused the thought that it would have been better to have
been hung. At night, the hatches were screwed down and the
prisoners left to fight among themselves in the wretched candlelight or, when the tallow had run out, the claustrophobic darkness.

And yet in some ways he had been granted some good fortune. Usually newcomers were relegated to the lowest deck and
if their stamina lasted and they didn't succumb to gaol fever,

they then progressed to the middle deck. He had been housed in the second deck right from the first. Even so, it had been "hell on earth," as one prisoner had so aptly named it. Violent attacks from fellow prisoners were commonplace and even the slightest offense was punished by a whipping from the guards. A person always had to be wary, for there was no one who could be trusted. It was everyone for themselves with no thought to kindness. Whatever remained of innocence or honesty, it was certain to be lost in the dark depths of the prison ship. Even death was not held sacred. Like vultures, the other prisoners fluttered about to see if the "stiff" had anything at all of value on him.

"Rats, filth, and starvation," he said with a sigh. Oh, to be out of here, to be free.

Closing his eyes, he thought of Beth. If only he had stayed with her that day. If only he hadn't been caught. If only . . .

As if somehow intruding on her own thoughts, he heard a man's voice whisper "freedom." The men's whispering took up the chant and Jamie could only wonder what was going on. The cries were taken up by the women.

"The drunken sot o' a gaoler. He forgot to screw down the hatch and lock the holds when 'e left. It's our chance, yer blokes!"

"We're going ter break free!" yelled one prisoner. It was an uprising.

"Perhaps we won't be going to Botany Bay after all."

That thought jolted Jamie out of his lethargy. There was going to be a mutiny! He stood up and was pushed and shoved as the prisoners fought their way through the narrow entrance way. Then somehow he had made it to the upper deck.

All the prisoners were running to and fro, stealing small boats and pushing them into the sea. Others were jumping overboard. The churning ocean offered two alternatives—freedom or death. Did he want to take the chance? For a long moment he stood by the railing looking into the sea. If he didn't jump then he would spend the rest of his days in a foreign land.

"Kill 'im! Kill 'im, I saiy."

Jamie whirled around. It was the captain, however, about whom the men were speaking. Holding a gun to his head, they were evil and threatening.

"No, don't kill him," Jamie pleaded. "The suffering we go through isn't any of his doing."

"Wot would yer know about it?" One of the men was surly, squinting at Jamie as if he viewed him as his enemy.

"He just runs the ship. Leave him be! Murder never solves anything." In a bold show of bravery, Jamie reached out and grabbed for the gun. His reward was a stinging blow to the head.

"Shoot the captain. Shoot them both!"

There was a shot. Jamie felt a sting of pain in his shoulder. He recoiled, watching helplessly as the captain suffered a like fate only to be pushed over the side, his scream cutting the air.

Pulling himself up, he was poised atop the railing for only an instant. It was obvious the captain was unconscious. He would drown. It wasn't his business, or was it?

Without answering his own questions, he jumped—down, down, down, to be swallowed by the icy waters. The turbulent sea tugged him under as he swam frantically toward the blue-clad form.

Beth stared at the man from Scotland Yard in disbelief. She couldn't believe it! Jamie in Newgate?

"He's alive, or so you might call it, though I have no doubt but that he's been going through hell."

"How did you find out?"

"From a prison turnkey. An informant."

"Newgate!" She covered her mouth with her hand to silence a scream. It took a moment for her to regain her composure. She had found him. She had found Jamie. As long as he was alive, there was always hope of getting him free. Somehow! A new trial perhaps, this time with a lawyer of her choosing.

It was cold outside the tenement, with a brisk wind that whipped at Beth's hair as she walked along clutching at her cloak.

Still she stubbornly refused to hire a carriage. She wanted to walk, to let her feet skim over the cobblestones. She knew just where she was going. Newgate.

Sixteen

Newgate! The most loathsome place in London. Oh, how the very sight of it chilled her blood with dread. Jamie was here! Of all places. Oh, if only she had known sooner. If only she had guessed.

"It will take quite a sum of money, Miss Longley, to free this young man. Are you prepared to pay the fee?" The lawyer looked at her skeptically, as if to ask what this man meant to her.

"I don't care how much money it takes," she answered sternly. Anxious to get on with it, she led the way. She wondered if she could trust this man. So many lawyers, magistrates, turnkeys, and parish beadles were corrupt that one never really knew whom to trust.

"Then I'll talk to the magistrate." He grimaced as he withdrew a snowy-white linen handkerchief from the inside pocket of his dun-colored coat. Take this, my dear, no doubt you will have need of it." At her questioning look he said, "You will find the stench nearly unbearable, at least until we get beyond the *common* prisoners."

The heavy spiked doors swung open with a groan and Beth followed the lawyer inside. From where they stood behind the wicket, she could see prisoners being admitted, watched in fascinated horror as tattered individuals were transported to their cells in prison carts.

"Poor souls!"

"Hardly my dear. Criminals every last one or they would not be here." The lawyer patted her arm.

She stiffened, hurrying to Jamie's defense. "I'm sure that's not true about all," she said, shuddering. Beth had thought herself prepared for what she'd find behind the prison bars, but she was wrong. It was like glimpsing Dante's *Inferno*.

Silently, she traversed the endless corridors and descended the steeply winding staircases. This was the place where Jamie had spent his days while she had been living in splendor, she thought, guilt squeezing at her insides. Dear God, if she had only known.

As she walked along, her eyes searched in the dim light, staring through the grates for a glimpse of Jamie's face.

"Disgusting animals. Savages." The lawyer mumbled into his handkerchief. "I don't know why I chose such the occupation as this. Better to have been a merchant, I dare say."

"My father was a merchant," Beth murmured, touched by the deprivation that she saw. The gaunt faces and wild hopeless eyes of those who somehow managed to push their faces against the grating gave her insight into what they were suffering. She could feel their misery and mourned for them.

"A merchant? Is that so?" As Beth paused he put his hand in the small of her back and gave her a nudge. "Come along. The prisoner you seek has been lodged in far more comfortable quarters."

"Different quarters?" Beth breathed a sigh of relief. Jamie was living more comfortably then than these poor souls. "Nonetheless, I want him out of here!"

"As you request." The lawyer resumed his gait, coming at last to a large burly guard. "The thief, Jamie Morgan. We are here to see him."

With a grunt the turnkey obeyed, slamming the door behind him.

Beth watched the guard go and was consumed with impatience. She wanted Jamie out of here as quickly as possible. Hopefully he wouldn't have to have another trial. Jamie here. It was still hard to believe.

"Jamie, is it?"

The lawyer's scrutinizing eyes made Beth afraid to say more.

Something about the man cautioned her to be wary. Too much said might be dangerous. What was important now was that Jamie knew she would soon set him free. Oh, how she wished she could throw her arms about him, to hug him and kiss him and tell him how much she missed him and loved him.

"This might take a while. You must be prepared," the lawyer said matter-of-factly.

"I'm prepared for anything," Beth whispered, or at least she thought that she was. Still, when the guard came back, and told her Jamie had been transferred to a convict ship headed far across the seas, she nearly fainted.

"No!" Banging on the bars, she wouldn't believe.

"Come along Miss Longley, or you'll find yourself in here, too." The lawyer pulled her along, back through the halls and stairs through which they had come. At last the suffocating depths of Newgate were behind her.

Jamie's lungs were burning for want of air, the heavy body of the captain was weighting him down. Still, he wouldn't let the man go. He had gone this far in trying to save his life. He wasn't about to give up now. Kicking his legs furiously to propel his body upward, he was rewarded when he reached the surface. Gulping in the sweet air, he prepared himself for another assault.

The waves were furious, throwing him back and forth like two gigantic hands. Several feet away he could see three other forms struggling against the sea. He could hear their shrieks of fright, watched helplessly as they were sucked under. Then he was struggling in the icy darkness again.

The water was so cold that it drained what meager strength he had and yet he wouldn't give in to death. Not his, and not the man whose life he had saved.

"If I can only hold on a little longer."

Strange, he thought, but the less he fought the water the fewer times it took hold of him. With that thought in mind he ceased fighting the ocean and tried to work with the rhythm of the rolling water.

He wanted to survive so desperately. It wasn't his time to die, he vowed. He was needed! Beth! The thought of her gave him renewed strength. But how long could he survive in these waters? The shore seemed to be miles away.

Up and down, rising and falling, he held fast to the ship's captain as he let himself drift with the waves, saving what strength he could. Could he somehow maneuver himself toward land? He doubted it. It was too far away. His only hope lay in attracting the attention of one of the fishing boats in the harbor.

"Help me! Help! Help!" He cried out over and over, his voice being drowned out by the thunder. Still, he was persistent. He hadn't survived Newgate and the ocean's depths without reason. "Help me!"

The shadowy form of a boat loomed more than a hundred feet ahead. Taking a deep breath, he opened his mouth to scream but a wave sent a froth of water and in the end he came up choking. For one agonizing moment he feared that all was lost, but gathering all his strength, he shouted out as loud as he could.

"What's that, Davie?"

"A shout?"

"Someone's out there."

"In the ocean. Don't be daft!"

They both listened, hearing it again.

"Let's follow that sound. Pull on the oars, Davie."

Jamie's watery prison seemed endless. Having swallowed some of the ocean's water he felt sick to his stomach and choked back the bile that rose in his throat. The boat was moving closer! If he could just hold on to his strength a little longer . . .

"There. In the water. It looks like a man. No, two!" There was a long pause, then strong hands pulled Jamie and the man he had rescued from the water.

"Thank God!"

He felt exhilarated with the feel of solid wood beneath him as he was yanked into the boat. Lying in an exhausted sprawl of arms and legs, he closed his eyes.

"What on earth are you doing out here?"

"The ship . . . a mutiny. I jumped overboard to save him." Jamie pointed.

"A prison ship." The men now were wary. "Who are you? Are you one of the convicts?"

"No! Please!" For just a moment he thought of jumping into the ocean again. He couldn't bear being put aboard that ship again. Better by far to let the ocean claim him.

"Oh, Davie, look what you've done." One of the men seemed to be on Jamie's side. "He could just as well be one of the guards." The man winked at him. "Besides, the magistrates of London haven't always been fair to us. We owe no loyalty to them."

Jamie had no other choice but to trust them. He closed his eyes once again. He was shivering from the chill but he was covered with a soft piece of canvas. The waves were rocking the fishing boat, back and forth. Back and forth. Jamie lost all track of time as he lay huddled and quaking with cold on the hard wooden boat floor. Darkness enveloped him in a cloud of sleep.

Beth's face paled. There had been a prison riot on the Sea Horse, the boat Jamie was on. Fifty or more inmates had escaped the confines of the ship, twenty or more had jumped overboard and were thought to have drowned. Every newsboy on every corner in London was shouting out the story.

Hurriedly, she sought out her lawyer. He was sitting at a desk, piles of documents piled in front of him as usual. Hunched over the papers, he was scribbling something with his pen.

"What about Jamie Morgan? What has happened to him?" Outside she was calm but inside she was trembling.

"I have been trying desperately to get him released." The lawyer shifted uncomfortably in his chair. "The judge seems loath to admit he might have made a mistake in sentencing an innocent party."

"Still, I want him pardoned."

"Pardoned!" The lawyer snapped his fingers. "Just like that? By God, Miss."

"I want to get him out."

A shiver stole over Beth's skin as she remembered her visit to Newgate. The prisoners were mixed together—young and old, the beginner with the experienced offender, the accused with the condemned, the transports with those under sentence of death— all crowded together in one promiscuous assemblage—a noisy, idle, clamorous throng, begging at the bars of the prison with spoons attached to the ends of sticks or fighting wretchedly among themselves.

"Be that as it may, Miss. These things take time."

"And in the meantime Jamie has been taken aboard that rat-infested ship. Well, I will hold you responsible if anything disastrous happens."

"All right then."

The lawyer hustled her off in a carriage to Newgate. There they learned the details of the transport ship mutiny. Jamie was one of the missing.

"We've apprehended those responsible for the uprising," one of the gaolers blurted, "and we have a list o' the missing. Most likely in Davy Jones's locker now they be." Taking off his cap, he showed a grudging display of respect, putting it to his breast as if at a funeral.

"I want to know for certain."

Beth and the lawyer sought out the judge with that intent in mind. Picking up the piece of paper, he hastily scanned the names. "I ought to have you thrown into prison yourself, Sir, just for barging in like this. I will. If it ever happens again."

There was no mistaking the astonishment etched on his face, an expression that made Beth stare at him apprehensively. "What is it?"

"Jamie Morgan is listed. He was seen jumping over the ship's railing and since then . . ."

"Since then?" Beth called upon every ounce of self-control she possessed.

Shaking his head, the judge seemed sympathetic for the first time. "He has not been found. It appears, my good man, that he has drowned."

Beth stared at the judge, her eyes misting. "Dear merciful God!" Bitter despair enveloped her. Jamie was gone! Dead! All this time she had managed to keep her hope alive that he would hold her in his arms again, that all would have a happy ending, but there was no justice! Only blind, stubborn fools.

"Take me home." She was through hoping. All she knew was that there was no point to her life if he did not share it. No joy in the days that stretched ahead.

Seventeen

The hospital ward was dimly lit. There was just enough lamp-light to illuminate the forty cots carefully laid out in rows. A fire burned in the corner but it did not give off enough heat to warm the room.

It was raining outside. The dampness seeped through the walls and dribbled from holes in the ceiling. The drip, drip, drip of rain as it spattered into pewter pots merged with the cries and groans of the poor unfortunates laid out on the sodden mattresses.

"How is this one going, Matthew?" the gray-haired doctor asked as he scribbled on a pad of paper.

"He's out cold. I gave him some laudanum for the pain. Suffered a gunshot wound and swallowed enough sea water to kill an ordinary man."

The doctor prodded at the patient. "I can see that he's been sewn." He looked annoyed when blood from the oozing cut got on his hands. With a grunt, he wiped them on his already dirty brown frock coat.

"Aye, that he has. One of the nurses did it."

"Hmmm. Do we know who he is?"

"No. There was a prison riot aboard the ship."

"Riot?"

"Aye. It's thought he might be one of the convicts."

The doctor stepped back. "Convict!"

Matthew held up his hand. "Aye, but listen. There was another man with him. The captain of the Sea Horse. Took a bullet to the head. Would have died but this one saved him. You might jolly well say he's a hero."

"Hero indeed." Again he made a notation.

"Does he have any relatives? Anyone to claim the body if he dies? Or will it just be one more for a pauper's grave?"

"The officials from Newgate said there was no one," Matthew answered, "but he does keep calling out a name. Beth. Beth, he says over and over."

"Beth?"

"It sounds like Longley. Beth Longley." Matthew stared down at the patient. "Listen, you can hear him."

"Beth . . . Beth." Jamie opened his eyes. He saw two men staring down at him. He looked from one to the other. Who were they? Where was he? Painfully, he tried to remember. "Beth."

He felt helpless. Weak. He had lost a lot of blood. He touched his shoulder.

I have to get away! They'll send me back to Newgate. I must . . . He sat up, only to fall back down as darkness closed in on him.

"He's out like a light again." Matthew clucked his tongue. " 'Tis a pity." He tugged on the doctor's sleeve. "What shall we do with him? We're running out of beds."

The doctor shrugged his shoulders. "Send him back to Newgate."

"Newgate?" Matthew shuddered. "Somehow it doesn't seem fair. Not after what he did." Watching the doctor leave, he shook his head. "No, it doesn't seem fair." Hunkering down, he gently shook the injured man, hoping beyond hope that he could somehow locate the mysterious "Beth."

The cold rain which had been drizzling all day was beginning to pour down in earnest. Beth merged with the throng walking down the cobbled streets, bombarded with raindrops. Even so, she refused to seek comfort and shelter. Jamie was alive! He'd been found. She was on her way to see him and nothing, not even a flood, could slow her down.

"Jamie!"

Frantically, she ran toward the door of the hospital, not even stopping until she had pushed inside. Standing in the doorway, she was soaking wet, her hat totally ruined, her hair a mass of tight ringlets.

"Who?" Matthew knew somehow. "Beth."

Beth looked around with a shudder. The hospital room was filthy. The plaster walls were stained with blood and dirt. There was dust everywhere. The wooden floors looked as though they had never been mopped despite the large pail of water and the mop that stood in the corner. The sheets on the beds looked as if they hadn't been changed in weeks, if ever.

She looked down. "Jamie."

The flickering flames of the lamp illuminated the face of the man lying on the rumpled cot. Dear God, it really was Jamie. But he looked so crushed and broken and pathetically thin. What had they done to him? Beth was shaken to see a man once so virile and strong now reduced to a wounded being. Bending down, she gently wiped the caked blood from his face with her handkerchief, cursing the villainy that had brought him down.

"He's been whispering your name over and over. I'd hoped we would find you." Seeing that she was well-dressed, the doctor's attitude changed to one of extreme deference.

"Well, now you have," she whispered. She bent down. "Jamie! Jamie!"

His arms and chest were well-muscled and she remembered their strength when he had held her. A tuft of black hair covered his broad chest and trailed in a line down to his navel. Only a bloodstained bandage marred his perfection.

"Jamie . . ."

"Warmth. Warmth and light. Everything was sort and safe." He could sense that someone was with him but he hadn't the

strength to open his eyes. Instead, he gave himself up to the
sensations. Bit by bit an encompassing warmth was stealing the
cold from his body.

"Jamie. Jamie . . ."

A voice was whispering in the darkness. A comforting, familiar voice. Fingers as comforting as a soft spring breeze were
touching him. Up. Down. Across his chest. The icy core inside
him began to thaw. It was almost as if he could feel the blood
coursing through his veins.

"Come back to me, Jamie . . . The world without you will be
much too lonely . . ."

A voice calling to him, pleading with him.

Slowly he opened his eyes and the vision he saw was a walk
in the sun. "Beth!" Was it a dream? He had seen her face so
often only to find out it was just an illusion.

I'm here." She took his hand.

He felt the warmth of her flesh, the firmness of her grip. It
was real! "Beth!"

For the first time in a long while he was at peace.

Epilogue-1851

The sun looked like a golden coin, balancing on the dark glow of the waters. Standing at the railing of the ship, Beth looked out across the land mass, focusing on her new home. America! Like nowhere else on earth, or so she had been told.

"Far away from London. What do you think? Will we be happy here?" Jamie put his arm around her, drawing her against his chest.

"I'd be happy anywhere with you. Besides, from what I have heard, this is the land of opportunity."

She and Jamie were beginning a whole new life in a new land with no more fears of the past. Because of his heroism, Jamie had been given a pardon and a monetary reward, besides. With that money and the money she had inherited from Catherine Claremont they had bought a small plantation in Florida, a place known for its bright sunny days all year 'round.

Together they watched as the anchor was dropped, the boat secured, and the gangplank put in place. They were here! In some ways it was unbelievable. Certainly the voyage had been fraught with moments when she had feared she would never reach land. First she was stricken with sea sickness. Then there had been a storm that had nearly upended the ship. Lightning, booming thunder, and huge waves had made even the bravest on board wail in fear. Yet somehow, the steamer had stayed afloat. Now, as Beth looked down at the peaceful waters, it seemed as if it had been little more than a nightmare.

"Is this your luggage, Miss?"

Beth nodded. "Mine and my husband's."

With a loving smile, her eyes appraised him from the corner of her eye. His shirt molded to his arms and upper body, emphasizing his physique. His virile power deeply stirred her as he reached out to hold her in his arms. It was hard to believe the agonizing days it had taken him to fully recover his strength— Weeks in which she had never left his side. But her love had worked magic.

"America," Jamie whispered. "Who would have believed it?"

They stood together at the railing, taking pleasure in being together, calmly and unhurried as the rest of the crew and passengers scurried about.

Jamie thought how complete his life was now that he had Beth to share it. His hands moved along her back, sending shivers of pleasure up her spine. For an endless time he held her to him. Then his mouth covered hers, his lips tracing the outline of hers with feathery kisses, his tongue stroking the edge of her teeth. His lips played seductively on hers.

Yes, they belonged together for now and for all time, Beth thought, wrapping her arms around his neck. The captain of the ship had married them that morning. Tonight, their first night together in America, was going to be their honeymoon.

"I really do belong to you now, Jamie. Now and for evermore . . ."